# ZOMBIE
# BLONDES

# ZOMBIE BLONDES

## BRIAN JAMES

SQUARE FISH

FEIWEL AND FRIENDS

NEW YORK

To my mother

SQUARE
FISH

An Imprint of Macmillan

ZOMBIE BLONDES. Copyright © 2008 by Brian James. All rights reserved.
Printed in April 2009 in the United States of America by RR Donnelley,
Harrisonburg, Virginia. For information, address Square Fish,
175 Fifth Avenue, New York, NY 10010.

Square Fish and the Square Fish logo are trademarks of Macmillan and
are used by Feiwel and Friends under license from Macmillan.

Library of Congress Cataloging-in-Publication Data
James, Brian,
Zombie blondes / by Brian James.
p. cm.
Summary: Each time fifteen-year-old Hannah and her out-of-work father move she
has some fears about making friends, but a classmate warns her that Maplecrest,
Vermont's cheerleaders really are monsters.
ISBN: 978-0-312-57375-1
[1. Moving, Household—Fiction. 2. Fathers and daughters—Fiction.
3. High schools—Fiction. 4. Schools—Fiction. 5. Cheerleading—Fiction.
6. Cliques (Sociology)—Fiction. 7. Popularity—Fiction. 8. Zombies—Fiction.
9. Vermont—Fiction.] I. Title.
PZ7.J153585Zom 2008    [Fic]—dc22    2007050869

Originally published in the United States by Feiwel and Friends
Square Fish logo designed by Filomena Tuosta
First Square Fish Edition: 2009
10 9 8 7 6 5 4 3 2 1
www.squarefishbooks.com

# ZOMBIE
## BLONDES

**There aren't any rules to running away from your problems.** No checklist of things to cross off. No instructions. *Eeny, meeny,* pick a path and go. That's how my dad does it anyway because apparently there's no age limit to running away, either. He wakes up one day, packs the car with everything we own, and we hit the road. Watch all the pretty colors go by until he finds a town harmless enough to hide in. But his problems always find us. Sometimes quicker than others. Sometimes one month and sometimes six. There's no rule when it comes to that, either. Not about how long it takes for the problems to catch up with us. Just that they will— that much is a given. And then it's time to run again to a new town, a new home, and a new school for me.

But if there aren't any rules, I wonder why it feels the same every time. Feels like I leave behind a little bit of who I was in each house we've left empty. Scattering pieces of me in towns all over the place. A trail of crumbs dotting the map from everywhere we've left to everywhere we go. And they don't make any pictures when I connect dots. They are random like the stars littering the sky at night.

"You're gonna like this place . . . you really are," my dad says over the song that goes in and out of static on the radio. Taking his eyes off the road for a second to give me the goofy smile he saves for when he's trying to cheer me up. A soft tap of his hand on my knee until I stop staring out the car window and look at him.

"I liked the last place . . . and the place before that one, too," I snap, pouting at him out of the corner of my eye. It's the look I save for when I want him to leave me alone. I'm not in the mood for cheering up. I'm sick of moving. I'm sick of being the new girl all the time. And I'm sick of my dad trying to make it sound like some exciting adventure every time we run out of money to pay rent and have to cut out of town like criminals.

I sink down in my seat and press my forehead against the window. The leaves have all changed and the orange ones seem to mix with the brown and yellow ones like the tail of a comet in some cartoon as we speed by. The branches dance in the wind and wave the leaves about. Waving good-bye as the mile markers flash past and then we're gone. Another minute closer to the middle of nowhere. Another mile closer to Maplecrest, the town my dad swears I'm going to like.

"Are you looking at the mountains? Aren't they beautiful?" he asks, his eyes beaming as he looks from peak to peak rising in front of the windshield.

I don't answer because I'm not speaking to him.

It's my new approach since he doesn't seem to listen to me. Maybe if I don't say anything, he'll get the message that I'm mad. I'm not even sure why. I mean it's never bothered me so much before. The moving-around thing. We've been doing it ever since my dad stopped working regularly. Or ever since they said he wasn't able to work, I should say. Since I was ten years old. So almost six years now. Long enough that I should be used to it. And I am, it's just that I really did like the last place. I made friends for the first time in a long time. And he promised me when we went there that it would be the last time I'd have to start over.

It was my fault for believing him, I guess.

He's told me that promise before. "It's gonna be different this time, you'll see." He's said it so often that I think he almost believes it. He always says it as we're pulling into our new driveway. I always roll my eyes and tell him, "Sure thing," because I know nothing will change. Nothing ever does. It's not that he doesn't try. He does. He'll take a job he hates because he can't do the one he likes. He can't be a cop again, not after what happened in the city when he used to be one. He says the memories are too painful. That's why we ran in the first place, ran from the city to out here in the middle of nothing. And I don't have the heart to tell him that it hasn't helped. Six years and we're still running and he's still taking jobs that make him miserable. He'll take another one once we get to Maplecrest. Then he'll get fired because he can't stand it. We'll eat noodles and rice for a few weeks and then one day I'll come home from school and the car will be packed up with everything we own and it will start all over again.

That's why I've changed my mind about there not being any rules. Because there is one rule to running away from your problems. The one that says it will repeat itself over and over again like the seasons or the sunset or the chains of fast-food restaurants that we pass, going from one place to the next. It always comes back to the same thing. I always find myself sitting in the passenger seat of our car, biting my nails and wondering if my new high school will be better or worse than the last.

"Looks like this is our stop," my dad says as we pass a sign directing us to turn off the highway. It's his way of telling me to roll down my window and stick my arm out to let the cars behind us know we're turning since our blinkers don't work.

The wind rushes in the open glass and I lazily put out my hand and point. My dad tells me I'm the best copilot ever to navigate the winding roads of Vermont. He's trying to be cute and so I try even harder to be sour as I look at him with a sulky expression.

"Come on, Hannah, don't be like that," he says, nudging me in the side.

"How do you want me to be? My hand is freezing and your jokes aren't funny," I say as the car slows down and he turns the steering wheel. I pull my hand back in and roll up the window and instantly miss the noise of the wind rushing in because the return of quiet means he's going to say something else and I've been trying my best not to speak to him.

"Don't be so dramatic," he says in a tone of voice he uses to tell me I'm being unfair.

"Dramatic is moving your daughter to the middle of nowhere every few months," I correct him, giving him the smug smile he hates so much in order to let him know that I've only just begun to be unfair.

But I guess even I can't spoil his mood because he doesn't take the bait. He doesn't argue with me. In fact, he actually laughs! It makes me so mad that I want to scream, but he seems so happy that I can't even work up the energy to stay angry enough to get anything out. It's impossible to yell at him when he has that silly smile on his face and pats me on the shoulder. I've never been able to stay mad at him for longer than a few hours at a time before, and I feel myself caving. God, sometimes I hate him for being so hard to hate!

I turn back to the window.

It's easier being miserable if I don't look at him.

I watch as our new hometown rolls past.

"Maplecrest," I mutter to myself, reading the name off the sign as we turn onto the street that splits the town in half. It even sounds boring. And as we drive through, it's just as I pictured—a lot of nothing. One pharmacy. One diner. A bank and my school and that's about it. It'd be a miracle if anything exciting ever happens in this place.

"Isn't this great!" my dad says, taking it all in. It's just the kind of time-warp town he loves. Nothing's changed in it since the time when he was a kid. Or even before that. Looks like a town from a movie that's too boring to even sit through long enough to figure out what the story is about.

Apparently I'm not the only one who thinks that, either, because there are FOR SALE signs up all over the place. Every third or fourth lawn at least. No wonder we're able to live here. Even we aren't poor enough to be chased from a ghost town.

"Yeah, Dad, you were right. I love it already," I say sarcastically. The only good thing about this place is that I'm sure we won't be staying long. With this many people moved out, that means there's no jobs. Empty houses equals no work. It's the one economics lesson I've learned from being shuffled about my whole life. We'll be gone before Thanksgiving, I guarantee it. So long, Maplecrest, I hardly knew you!

My dad tells me to keep an eye out for street signs. Says we're looking for Walnut Cove. I spot it right away. "It's up there," I tell him, glad it's on the left so that I don't have to embarrass myself right away by being the car's turn signal.

Ours is the fifth house we come to. There's nothing special about it. It's small and brown on the outside. Some trees in the yard and the lawn is grown over, wild with weeds. Looks like it hasn't been cut in months and the leaves need raking. Another in a long line of houses we've lived in. Its windows as blank as the eyes of strangers and most likely will feel the same to me on the day we pull out.

The gas light in the car goes on as we ease into the driveway. My dad looks at the dashboard and smiles. "It's a sign," he says. "We're home."

"It's a sign that we're broke," I say, gripping the handle and kicking the door open. I take a quick look around. An empty house across the street. Another one two doors down. The mountains in the background like a wall fencing us into this crappy town. I take a deep breath and get myself ready to start all over again.

As I reach into the backseat to get my bag out, my dad comes around and puts his arms around me. "It won't be so bad," he says. And though I want to pretend like he's being selfish, I know he's not. I can hear it in his voice. I always hear it. I know how sorry he is for putting me through this and that's why I try my best not to take it out on him.

"I know," I say, spinning around and giving him a half-hearted smile. I can sense the words forming in his mind and I put my hand up to his mouth to keep them in. "Just don't promise me anything this time, okay?" I say. He nods and lets go of me. I can tell it hurts his feelings, but I just can't stand to hear him say it again.

I grab the bag that holds most everything I own. The pink one with the flower patches sewn on, and I let them drag along the ground as I drag the bag to the front door. My dad comes up behind me with the key in his hand. "We still a team?" he asks.

"Sure, Dad. We're still a team," I say and do my best to try and not look miserable.

# ONE

I can usually pick out the popular kids soon after setting foot into a new school. The girls, anyway. They wear popularity like a uniform for everyone to see. From their hairstyles to their expensive shoes. Everything about them is torn from the glossy pages of the latest teen fashion magazines. Everything about them is perfect. At least on the outside, anyway.

The boys are a little trickier.

Their looks have only a small part to play in deciding their place in the social order of things. What they're into is just as important as how they look. Depends on what kind of school it is, too. There are as many different kinds of high schools as there are different kinds of cliques in each one. There's the artsy sort of schools where the skinny, mysterious boys are the ones who get all the attention. Then there's the college-prep kind of schools where class rank and GPA go hand in hand with a boy's cute looks to determine where he stands with the girls. At thug schools and drug schools, the more damaged or dangerous a boy is makes all the difference. Last, but not least, there're jock schools like Maplecrest where all that really counts is how good a guy is at sports. Even if he's zit faced and moronic, a boy can be popular here, so it could take some time to figure it all out.

But with girls it doesn't matter so much what kind of school it is. It's always the thinnest, prettiest ones wearing the least amount of clothing that the dress code allows who rule the hallways. Because boys' tastes don't change much just because they like painting more than sports. So it's always the girls pretty enough to put on a postcard that get to be one of the Perfect People. The social elite. The clique that runs the school. The ones who get away with everything by batting their eyelashes and pretending not to know any better. They get to decide which of the other girls are okay to talk to and which should be teased into having an eating disorder.

Different schools but always the same thing.

Those are the girls I need to impress if I want to be popular, or keep from pissing off if I just wish to fit in. That makes figuring out who they are pretty important. Highest priority if I wish to avoid making a mistake that will get me on the wrong list unintentionally. A dirty look is all it takes. It's the way it's been at every school I've passed through in the last couple of years, so I've gotten pretty good at figuring out who they are. My social well-being depends on it.

Maplecrest might be the easiest school yet.

I know who the most popular girl is the second I see her.

One look is all it takes. Her long blond curls like a halo when the sunlight shines on her just right. Perfect smile and perfect skin like an angel made of porcelain. Sparkling blue eyes with soft pink eyelids to match the strawberry pout of her upper lip. The slender curve of her shoulder and fragile shape of her knees peeking out from the bottom of her short skirt. She's delicate like a bird as she glides through the cafeteria. Every pair of eyes following her as she soars to the table crowded with other pretty girls who just look like lesser clones once she joins them.

I don't need to know her name or anything about her to know she's the It Girl in school. It's written all over the faces of her friends as they wait their turn for her to say hi to them. Each and every one trying so hard to look exactly like she does. Each of them pretty, too. Each of them wearing the same bleached hair and bleached skin but with a little less twinkling in their eyes, making them a little less perfect.

And even though I promised myself I wouldn't do it this time, I start comparing myself with them, the Perfect People. I can't help it. I have to know where I stand. Crummy town or not, I care what people think of me. It's a bad habit. My dad calls it teenage-girl sickness and says there's a cure for it. I tell him I know there is, but that I don't really want to end up being a crazy cat lady when I get older.

I twist my hair around my finger and stare at the split ends. Mine doesn't have the same shine and it's not nearly as blond. Mine's more like dirty straw than a golden halo. And my eyes are muddy, too, and look nothing like the sky the way the popular-table girls' do. All of them so blond and beautiful, like little figurines too precious to let children play with.

I push my tray away. I'm not hungry anymore.

It's not that I think I'm ugly or anything. I know I'm cute enough. And I don't want to be the prettiest girl in school or anything like that. It's just that I don't even come close. Not to their leader or even to her tagalongs. I thought in a small, time-forgotten town like this that I'd at least have a shot. It's not really that important to me, it's just that it's easier being new in a school if you're one of the prettiest girls. I hoped maybe this time I'd get lucky. But that dream vanished the instant I saw her.

"Her name's Maggie Turner," a voice says in my ear as if reading my thoughts. Not startling me enough to scream, but just enough to squeak like a little mouse.

I turn my head to see a scrawny-looking boy with shaggy straw hair dressed in shabby clothes. I recognize him from one of my classes. Takes me a second to place him. Geometry, third period. The kid a few rows over who kept looking at me so much that I just stopped checking after a while. He's not so bad looking, but he's not exactly my type, either. Long and lanky and a little on the creepy side. And before I can make up my mind whether I want to tell him to get lost or not, he pulls up the empty chair and sits down next to me.

"Maggie Turner," he says again. "You're wondering what her name is, aren't you?" I'm not sure what to say. I wasn't really expecting company. First day in a new school mostly equals isolation, especially in the lunchroom. It's one of the symptoms of the new-kid disease. Everybody wants to talk about you, but nobody wants to talk to you. Not at first anyway and his surprise visit catches me off guard. Not to mention the fact that he knew what I was thinking about.

"I was just . . . ," I start to say but never finish.

"You were just staring at Maggie Turner like everyone else," he says and I can feel my face turning red.

It's not that I mind getting caught or that I'm embarrassed about being fascinated with the popular girls. I just don't know if I want to share it with some skinny, weird kid who wanders the lunchroom searching for girls he doesn't know to sit next to. But whatever the reason, my cheeks start to blush and he begins to notice.

"It's okay," he says. "She's an attention magnet. Everyone likes to stare at her." He puts his hands behind his head and leans back. Tilts the chair until it's resting against the wall and settles in like we're long-lost pals.

"Look, what do you want?" I ask in a snotty tone because at this point all I really want is for him to go away. I'd rather be lonely than sit with him. He sort of gives me the creeps. I even slide my chair a few inches away. Too bad he can't take a hint, though. He's either a little dense or else he has the beginnings of a crush on me. With my luck, it wouldn't surprise me. I'm never a magnet for attention so much as I'm a magnet for weirdos.

He puts his hands back on the table and lets the chair ease back down to the floor. Then he hunches over and leans closer to me like he's going to tell me a secret or something.

"Today's your first day, right?" he asks.

I'm not sure what that has to do with anything but I nod my head anyway.

"Well, I'm just trying to help you out, that's all," he says.

"Help me how?" I ask. I don't see him helping me out at all. The only thing he's doing is keeping any normal people from talking to me.

"I can tell you want to be friends with her," he says. I feel like arguing that I don't even know her and that he doesn't even know me, so how can he make that assumption. But deep down I know he's kind of right, so I don't bother. Besides, he knows he's right the same way I knew about Maggie being the It Girl in the first place. He can spot people like me just like I can spot the popular.

"So what if I do?" I ask him. "Is that a crime or something?"

"No," he says. "I just thought I'd try to save you from Maggie Turner's clutches before it's too late."

I can't help but smile a little, because I've seen this trick before. Get close to the new girl and scare her with tales of the evil clique. It's always the outsiders like him that try it. The malcontents. But that's all it is. A trick. Try to claim me for their own and poison me to the rest of the school. Still, though, he is sort of cute and he is the only person to talk to me all day, so I decide to humor him, anyway.

"Yeah, why's that?" I ask.

"Because Maggie isn't like the rest of us," he says in a whisper. Really getting into the part and looking around as if he's checking to make sure no one is listening. "She's not like real people, she's better. She was born on Christmas. Her favorite color is pink. Baby pink, not porno pink. And it doesn't matter how cold it is outside, she always wears short skirts and short tops and no one has ever once seen her shiver. She never eats anything but carrots, at least not in public. And though she doesn't have any proven super-powers, all her friends follow her like they're in some kind of cult. Plus, she just happens to be the captain of the cheer-leading squad and is one evil bitch on top of that."

I fold my arms across the table and rest my head. Open my eyes wide and give him all my attention like a little kid at story time. "You seem to know a lot about her for not liking her," I say with a little smile but I think the sarcasm escapes him.

"Everyone does, she makes sure of it," he says. No longer whispering and no longer playful like before. A little angry even as he taps the edge of the table with his knuckles.

"Let me guess," I say because it's my turn to play a little game with him. "Every boy has the hots for her, includ-ing you."

"Not me," he says without hesitating. Says it like a fact, never taking his eyes off her. Says it the way I can tell it's not just a denial. Says it so I know he doesn't just not like her, he despises her.

"But you did at one point," I say because I can tell that, too. "And she didn't like you, so now you hate her." No-body gives the kind of look he does to someone like Mag-gie Turner unless they're jealous or scorned. I can't see him being the kind of boy jealous of popularity, but he certainly looks like the emotional type who gets his feelings hurt.

I may have hurt them some, too, because he pushes his chair away from the table and half stands up. He's about to walk away but stops. Turns to me and opens his mouth and starts to stutter like he's not sure if he should say what he wants to. Then finally deciding to go ahead and say it, but refusing to take his eyes off the floor when he does. "It's just . . . you're kind of pretty . . . and she might try to turn you into one of them . . . one of her clones," he says. "I don't want to see that happen to you, that's all."

I tuck my lip under my top teeth.

"Is that supposed to be a compliment?" I ask.

"Nope," he says. "Just a warning."

I stare at him in silence and he stares back. Stares into my eyes for the first time since coming over to me. Something blank in his expression that doesn't make sense to me. He's either the most socially challenged boy I've ever met, or one of the cleverest. Whichever it is, he's by far the most interesting thing about this town so far.

He takes a step away before stopping. Makes a gesture like he forgot something and comes back. "My name's Lukas, by the way," he says.

"You know, you're really supposed to do that before you start pestering strange girls," I say.

"Yeah? Well, this is Maplecrest," he says.

"What does that have to do with anything?" I ask.

"You'll see," he says. "A lot of things in Maplecrest are done differently."

He starts to drift away again and this time I stop him. "Don't you want to know my name?" I ask him.

"It's Hannah," he says. Then he smiles for the first time. And I'm a little surprised, but he actually has kind of a sweet smile. "I was paying attention in class when the teacher called your name," he explains.

"Oh. Right," I say, remembering third period for the second time. "Well, thanks for the warning," I say with just enough attitude for him to know I'm not being completely serious.

"Do yourself a favor and stay away from them," he says with just enough attitude to let me know he's being deadly serious. Then he disappears into the crowd of faces, leaving me alone to listen to the million fragments of conversations happening all around me until the bell rings.

**The whispers start** the moment I sit down. Voices soft and slow from behind me. So quiet like trying not to make a sound but making sure I hear them just the same. The sound of syllables something like a hissing noise. Something like words slithering out from pointed tongues. A secret language mumbled behind hands held up to cover their mouths.

I don't have to know what they're saying to know it's about me.

I bite my lip and keep my eyes safely on my notebook because I know this is a test. I saw them watching me as I walked in. Hair so blond it would look white if it wasn't for their skin's snowy shade. The faint blue glow of electricity in the center of their eyes. Studying me. The way I walk. The way I dress. Everything about me, trying to figure out where I fit in.

The best thing for me to do is to ignore them. Despite what Lukas, the lunchroom boy, thinks, I'm aware of how mean popularity can make people. I've been through it enough times to be an expert. I know one wrong look in their direction could make me a gossip target for as long as I end up staying in this place.

When the whispers fade away, I hear them shuffle in their seats. Hear the sound of their shoes moving across the floor, coming toward me. Then the scent of vanilla perfume lingers over my shoulder and I brace myself, waiting to find out my fate.

"Hey, new girl?" one of them says and I turn my head to look up at where they're standing above me.

"Hey," I say. My voice coming out smaller than I planned and they seem to notice. Giggling a little at how nervous they make me.

"Your name's Hannah, right?" the other girl says and I nod. "Well, I'm Morgan," she says. "This is Miranda."

"Hi," I say, speaking quieter than I did before.

Miranda gives me a smug smile in response. Her hands firmly on her hips and her back arched slightly like an unfriendly cat. "We were just saying how much we really liked your bag," she tells me, her eyes darting down to take a quick glance at my backpack with the flower patches stitched into the fabric.

"Thanks," I say but without sounding happy about it. I don't dare take a look at my bag. I keep watching them instead. Searching for any signs of what's going to come next, because I can't help but feel like I'm being set up.

"Where'd you get it?" Morgan asks. I take a careful look at her before answering. There's nothing mean about her face. Innocent like an angel. A friendly smile on her lips, too, and I start to relax.

I'm overreacting.

It's that Lukas kid's fault for trying to spook me.

I start to breathe easier.

"I made it myself," I say. A little more sure of myself this time.

"Really? That's so cool!" Morgan says. Then she bends down to take a closer look. She traces the flower patches with her fingers and smiles at me. Asks me where I got them and if it was hard and I start to smile back. Tell her it wasn't that hard. Trying my best not to let on how proud I am about it.

"It couldn't have been *that* easy," Miranda says.

I glance over at her and see the start of a cruel smile. The pink skin under her eyes no longer looks gentle. Looks more like fire than flower petals, the way it looked before.

"I mean, you were probably in second grade or something, right?" she says. The words like the sound of an angry dog with sharp teeth.

They wait for my face to turn bright red before they start laughing. Wait for me to tuck my lip under my top teeth before they start to go back to their seats. Making sure I'm humiliated before leaving me alone.

"Can you believe she thought we were serious?" I hear Morgan say.

Miranda laughs and says she can believe it. "Anyone with a stupid little-girl bag like that would probably believe anything," she says.

I don't say anything because it was my fault for falling for it. I never should've let my guard down. It was stupid of me. I know better than that. But I really did believe her. She sounded so honest when she lied.

I push my bag under my desk with my feet. I knew it would make Morgan and Miranda snicker, but I didn't care.

I just wanted it out of sight. But I feel bad about it right away. The same way I used to feel when I'd hide my stuffed animals so my friends wouldn't know I still kept them. So I slide it back out into the row a tiny bit and try my best to ignore the laughter that starts up again a few desks behind me.

The whispers start all over again after that. Louder this time so that I can hear them clearer. Saying how cheap my clothes look. Saying they make me look homeless or something. I can feel my face turning redder as they rattle off insults like the whisper of bullets. Machine-gun whispers that only go silent when our English teacher walks in and begins to take attendance.

I listen as the names are read out loud. Watch hands shoot up in the air one after the other along with a chorus of "here" as the teacher goes through the alphabet. And I guess I should have listened to Lukas a little better. I should have stayed away from any and all cheerleaders.

My arm goes up when the teacher calls my name.

"Here," my voice escaping my lungs like a small cough.

The teacher pauses and looks up from the piece of paper in her hands. Narrows her eyes at me to memorize my face. "Welcome to Maplecrest, Hannah Sanders," she says, without sounding like she really cares at all before reading the next name.

I sink down in my desk.

There's no doubt that I've been welcomed, that's for sure. My two new best friends made sure of that. Made sure I knew exactly where I fit in. As a social outcast. The bottom of the food chain. Alone at the freak table, eating lunch with Lukas.

I watch the clock the rest of the period, counting the minutes until the day is over. Ignoring the rumors about me that spread from desk to desk like a disease. Spread through a series of hissing and laughter and dirty looks in my direction. I do my best not to let it show that it bothers me. Watching the clock and waiting until the moment I can disappear into the tide of kids flooding the hallway. Looking forward to being anonymous once again.

# TWO

My first day at Maplecrest High was hardly a success. Far from it, actually. Minus one creepy admirer and a perfect pair of stuck-up cheerleaders, no one even bothered to notice me too much. A few sideways stares is about all. I can't believe the kids in such a boring town would find me so dull. I guess I'm just more pathetic than I thought.

My dad says I just need to make more of an effort. "They'll come around once they get to know you." That's what he said yesterday after I got home and told him how much my day kind of sucked. It didn't exactly comfort me. I mean, that's what dads have to say. It's like a law of parenting that you have to think your own kid is special. It doesn't make much sense if you think about it, though. Every parent believes it, but it's a fact that not every kid is special. Somewhere along the way, some of them must be wrong.

My dad's bound to be one of them. Our lives are filled with his mistakes, so the chances are pretty good he's mistaken about me, too. It's quite possible that I'm no more interesting than the background noise of slamming lockers in the hallways.

I'm not ready to give up just yet, though.

Day two is more important than day one, anyway. At least I've always thought so. It's kind of like the dogs I used to watch in the park back when we lived in the city. The dogs would spend the first fifteen minutes just sniffing one another out before they made up their mind whether to play or fight. That's what the first day at a new school is like. Sniffing out the new dog. Day two is when they decide whether they want to play with me or chase me away.

Of course, I can make that choice, too.

I don't have to sit around and wait to be noticed, not on the second day. I can go up to them just as easily. I guess that's what my dad means by making an effort. But it makes more sense when I figure it out on my own. I just don't like him to be right, that's all.

"You can do this, Hannah!" I whisper to myself before taking a deep breath and closing my locker. Slinging my backpack over my shoulder and shoving my hands in my pockets, I step into the traffic of laughter and shuffling feet, passing through small groups of friends on my way into homeroom. Crossing my fingers deep inside my pockets, I scan the mostly empty desks for a friendly face.

My options aren't so great.

There's the dark-haired boy in the corner by the window. His hair's as black as midnight and I can see the dandruff flakes falling as he runs his hand through it each time he turns the page in the book that's only inches from his heavy glasses. Yeah. Not exactly my ideal vision of a best friend.

The two other choices don't get much better. The first one is asleep and the other is a mousy-looking girl with her hands folded across her desk like she's at church or something. Plus her makeup is like a little kid's playing dress up, heavy lipstick and blush in big circles like a circus clown's.

"Excuse me, I'd like to get by," a girl says as she taps my shoulder and turns her body to slip past where I'm blocking the doorway.

"Oh . . . sorry," I say and step aside. Only she steps in the same direction so that I step into her way. "Sorry," I stutter again, noticing the bleached shine of her hair for the first time. A cheerleader's smile to go with it.

She's one of them.

Perfect and popular and I just bumped into her like a clumsy freak. The backpack thing and now this! Strike two. Three strikes and their clique will hate me forever. So I tell her once more that I'm sorry and carefully step completely out of her way.

"Really, it's okay," she says. She smiles wider and shakes her head just enough to let me know that she means it.

"I was just . . . ," I start to say without any idea of what it was that I was just doing. "I don't know . . . daydreaming, I guess."

"It's not a big deal," she says. A second smile shows that she means it and that I can relax. She takes a few steps away before looking at me again. "Where are you sitting?" she asks.

I shrug my shoulders. "Nowhere yet."

"Sit here," she says. She points to a desk in the back row as she sits in the desk beside it. I can't help but wonder if this is another trick. Another set-up like Morgan's compliment on my bag the day before, but I don't dare turn down the invitation. Besides, she says it more like a command than an invitation.

I slide into the seat she's assigned me.

"What was your name again?" she asks. "I'm Meredith."

"Hi," I say. "I'm Hannah."

I bite my lip and try to think of something else to say. Nothing comes to mind, though, and I feel like an idiot sitting there staring at her. So I turn my head away and pretend to read the different banners and signs pinned onto the walls. Notices about upcoming pep rallies and football games. Meredith is busy fixing her hair in a little pocket mirror and doesn't seem bothered either way if I speak or not. And I know I'm blowing a chance to get in with her, but I can't help it. Not one interesting thing comes into my brain.

God!

Maybe I'm really just as boring as the mousy girl sitting in the front row!

I hear the click of her compact snapping shut and peek over as Meredith zips her purse closed. I can see her through the strands of my hair that hang across the side of my face. She's studying every part of me. I know she is. Checking for flaws and I wonder if I'd hear her snickering if one of her friends would be sitting next to her.

"So," she says to get my attention and I look over at her. I cross my fingers again, praying my face doesn't turn bright red as she looks me over carefully. "So, like what are you?" Meredith finally asks.

I open my mouth but no sound comes out.

No one has ever asked me a question like that before and I'm not sure how to answer. I'm not even sure I know what it means. "Um . . . ," I stutter and my tongue feels a few sizes too big as I stumble to come up with an answer.

Meredith laughs. It's not a mean kind of laugh, though. It's a misunderstanding sort of laugh as she changes the question around. "I meant, like what are you into? You're not like one of those girls who writes creepy poems about drowning or anything like that, are you?" she asks.

I shake my head.

"No," I say and I can see a faint sense of approval like a flash of lightning in the blue storm of her eyes.

"So what *do* you like?" her voice asks in the slow sound of a warning.

"I don't know," I say, shrugging my shoulders. "Normal things, I guess."

"Good," Meredith says. "I like normal things, too."

Then we both grin a little at how stupid we sound and things get easier from there now that we don't feel like strangers. She asks me what classes I have. I hand her my schedule, which I still keep close in my pocket to peek at before each class is dismissed so that I know where I'm going. She looks it over. Making faces as she reads the teachers' names. Making slightly more dramatic faces to let me know which teachers are truly awful and which are just the regular kind of annoying.

I keep silent and nod in agreement at everything she says.

That seems to please her enough to keep talking. Listening is just fine with me. It's better than being ignored.

School attendance duties put an end to our brief friendship, though. Our homeroom teacher narrows his eyes and grunts at the class for us to get quiet. Meredith and I shuffle our feet around to face the front of the room instead of each other as he calls out the first few names. The growl of his voice already seems less threatening than it did yesterday, simply because Meredith is sitting next to me. Because she talked to me.

Our teacher goes through the list without looking up once. Coughing out last names like they're something that makes him sick. He doesn't care to know any of the faces, just so long as they're *here*. I look over at Meredith and she rolls her eyes to let me know Mr. Edwards, our homeroom teacher, is one of those who belong in the truly awful category.

Everyone gets up at once, gathering up things when the bell dismisses us to first period. I toss my bag over my shoulder and step out into the row. I hesitate for a second, wondering if I should leave or wait for Meredith.

I decide to wait and she seems fine with it. We step into the hallway together but that's about as far as we get. She's met right away by a group of blondes who look nearly identical to her. I can still tell one of them apart from the rest, though. Because no matter how closely they resemble one another, Morgan stands out.

She doesn't bother to hide the evil look on her face as she squints at me, either. "Why are you talking to *her*?" she asks Meredith, saying it like I'm some kind of disease that needs to be avoided.

Meredith shrugs. "I wasn't really," she says.

I feel my stomach sink and my face blush. I lower my head and continue walking, hoping they don't notice. It's not like I really expected her to stick up for me or anything, but it still makes me feel like crap. It's my fault, though. One stupid conversation and I let myself think we might actually become friends.

"You better not," she sneers, "that girl's a freak."

I glance behind me just in time for one last nasty look from Morgan before they disappear into the tide of kids flooding the hallway.

So much for my day-two theory.

**Lukas is waiting** for me when I walk into the lunchroom. I see him sitting at the same table I sat at yesterday. But he's clever enough to try to hide it. Keeps his head down, buried in the bend of his arm like a kitten covering its face with a paw as it sleeps.

He's not fooling me, though. He could've sat anywhere else if he wanted to sleep. He sat there for me.

"Great," I sigh.

"I guess we're lunch buddies again?" I say, dropping my books on the table. The impact causes his body to jolt upright and he rubs his eyes to keep up the illusion that he'd somehow fallen sound asleep in the less than two minutes before I got there.

"Oh . . . hey," he yawns, stretching himself awake.

I roll my eyes at him and shake my head as I sit down in the seat next to his. "You know, it's pretty immature to fake like you weren't expecting me," I snap at him. I meant for it to put him on edge a little, but Lukas isn't bothered by it. He actually laughs and I wonder how such an outcast can be so confident.

"Well, I wasn't sure," he says. His eyes shine softly behind the greasy strands of his shaggy hair and he slouches over again to fold his arms across the table. "You never know. . . . I mean, they could've already made you into one of them," he says, nodding in the direction of Maggie Turner and her cheerleader clan.

I squint my eyes and look at him, trying to tell if he's teasing me or not. That's when I realize who he reminds me of. He's just like this character in a movie that I saw who sort of goes crazy and kills his best friend. I don't know why, but in a weird way it makes me like him a little more than I did before. I guess maybe because it makes him sort of interesting and since he's interested in me, that makes me sort of interesting, too.

"Nope," I say. "I'm still plain old me."

"I bet they've already scouted you out, though," he says. "Making sure you'll fit in if they decide to brain-wash you."

"Brainwash me? Give me a break," I say. I try my best to make it sound like I'm annoyed, but I can't help but glance over at the popular table where Meredith is gabbing away with the other girls. Our conversation plays back in my head, especially the part about her asking me what kind of things I was into.

Lukas doesn't miss it, either. "I'm right, aren't I?" he asks.

"Maybe," I say like it doesn't matter much. Secretly,

though, it kind of makes me smile on the inside. What if she was scouting me? It would mean that I at least have a chance of not ending up at the loser table for the rest of my days in Maplecrest. Of course, that daydream only exists if I make myself forget about Morgan.

Lukas makes a snide sort of huff and grumbles that he knew it would happen. "I told you," he says. His hands curl up into fists and he glares over at them like he's lost a game that no one else even knows they're playing. "Look, you got to stay away from them," he growls.

I can't figure out why it makes him so upset or why he even cares.

"Why?" I ask playfully. I can't help myself from teasing him a little. It's too easy. "What? Are you in love with me or something? Afraid they're going to steal me away and then we'll never be allowed to talk again?"

I watch his face turn all shy. Blinking his eyes. Glancing away so that I can't see how embarrassed he is. So I can't see that there's some truth to it. There's something cute about it, though. Something sweet about him when he's not being a total freak.

"It's not that," he says and exaggerates with a deep breath before and after he says it. Saying it like he thinks it's silly of me to even think it, but the way it comes out proves just the opposite.

"Well, what then?" I ask, not because I really want to know. I just feel a little bad about teasing him. So I twist around in my chair to face him. I give him my full attention and do my most sincere impersonation of someone who is listening carefully.

"It's just . . . they're dangerous, okay?" he says.

"Really?" I glance over at their table where the cheerleaders are sitting like delicate birds on a telephone wire and I wrinkle my forehead. "They don't look so dangerous."

Lukas pushes his chair back and stares into his lap instead of looking at me and I'm not sure what I did to get him so frustrated.

"I was just stating an obvious fact," I explain.

"Just forget it," he snaps.

"Whatever," I say. "It's forgotten."

He refuses to look up again. Twisting the strings of his sweatshirt around his finger over and over. Letting it drop and unwind before doing it all over again. I wait for a minute or so, waiting for him to come back to reality but he doesn't. He just sits there like a little kid who gets angry when no one wants to know his secret, only to go quiet when someone actually asks.

Fine with me.

I was only asking to be nice, anyway.

At least I can eat my lunch in peace now. That is, until he stops sulking and decides to tell me anyway. Tells me that Maggie and the rest of them are some kind of zombie cult and I nearly spit out my drink laughing because he's actually able to keep a straight face.

He doesn't say anything else.

He doesn't try to explain what he means.

He doesn't laugh along with me.

He doesn't do anything but sit there and start playing with the strings of his sweatshirt again. I make my face as serious as I can and watch him. Trying to get him to admit it's a joke, but he won't look at me.

"You might be the strangest person I've ever met," I tell him and he peeks over at me. I smile to let him know I mean it in a good way. And I do. Without him around, I'd probably die of boredom.

# THREE

Meredith is standing at her locker as I walk over to mine at
the end of the day. Our lockers are only two away from
each other and no one is at either of the ones that separate
them. Only a few feet of empty space between us. It feels
endless, though. Like the distance between oceans or the
space that keeps years from running into each other. And
like those things, it feels impossible for me to make the distance any smaller.

After this morning, I'm not sure I even want to.

But if I don't talk to her, maybe it'd seem rude.

Besides, it wasn't like she was mean to me or anything. I
just overreacted to what she said to Morgan, that's all. Morgan's the one who hates me for no reason. Not Meredith.
She was nice in homeroom. She'll probably be nice now, too.

But it doesn't matter how many times I tell myself that, my
stomach still starts to get nervous as I walk up to her. A belly

filled with butterflies as the empty space between me and her goes from two lockers to one. Then from one to none.

"Hi," I say.

It comes out of my throat sounding like a scratchy whisper and I wish I could take it back right away. The silence that comes from her makes me wish even harder that I'd kept quiet myself. Shifting my weight from foot to foot, standing there like a dork, counting the seconds going by, wondering how many I have to wait before I can walk away.

I'm only able to count to three, though, before Meredith turns around.

"Oh, hey," she says, putting the last book in her hand carefully on the shelf in her locker. "Hannah, right?" Squinting her eyes as she asks, but even though she says it like a question, I can tell she knows the answer.

"Right," I say. Then I bite my lip to hide the corny crooked smile from my face. She must think I'm so stupid. That's why she turns back to her locker, pretending to check if she needs anything else before she leaves.

"So?" she mutters, sounding slightly annoyed. "Good day?"

"Okay, I guess," shrugging my shoulders.

The afternoon sun drifts to our corner of the hallway and lingers on her for a moment as she turns back to me. Her features vanish in the glare. Her pale skin erased white so that her eyes burn blue. It makes me feel so imperfect standing next to her.

"Well, I have to go practice," she says, closing her locker.

"Yeah," I say. Not for any reason except that it seemed right to make some sort of sound. I turn my back and step over to my locker, relieved to get away.

"Hey?" Meredith says as I'm turning the combination on the lock. I glance over my shoulder and raise my eyebrows. Her blue eyes shine like a spotlight over me, moving up and down, looking at the way I stand and the way I dress, and I can't help but feel weird and shy. But then she smiles and it's like giving me approval, like saying I've passed some kind of test or something. "Have you thought about trying out for the squad?" she asks.

"Me?" I answer and she smiles. I shake my head. I hadn't thought about it. And I really don't think I would want to, but still I can't help but feel curious and also a little bit excited that she asked.

"Why not?" Meredith asks me, raising her voice in surprise. I suppose every girl in this little town has wanted to be one of them at some point. I guess if she waited a few days to ask, maybe I would have, too. "You should," Meredith says with a smile. Then she says she'll see me tomorrow. Turns around and I watch her disappear down the hall.


On my way out the building, a girl from one of my classes catches up behind me. She taps me on the shoulder and greets me with a friendly smile. "Hey, wait up!" she says and I begin to think that second-day stuff isn't such crap after all. "I think we're in sixth period together," she says.

If I wasn't still a little perked from Meredith's invitation, I'd most likely be defensive. Pretend I didn't know the girl tapping me. Act like I didn't remember that she sits behind me in history class. Pretend I didn't care. I'm glad I don't do any of those things, though, because she looks nice. A first potential best friend.

"Yeah, I think we are," I say. She holds up her hand, half waving as she's about to tell me her name's Diana. I interrupt her and tell her I already know. "I was cursed with a good memory," I tell her, borrowing a line from my dad. He's always said that he passed it down to me. A memory like a computer that can't forget things even if I wanted to. Most people forget half of everything they hear or see. Sure you lose some good times, but let's face it, most memories aren't so great and I think it might not be such a bad thing to be able to empty them every once in a while like the trash.

"I heard you talking to Meredith," Diana says and asks if I'm thinking about joining the squad. "It's none of my business, I'm just wondering." Her fingers move nervously inside her pocket like tiny spiders under her clothes and it slowly starts to come together.

The pink eye shadow that circles her dull green eyes.

The powder brushed on her face, poorly hiding a bad complexion.

A skirt not quite short enough. Hair not quite yellow enough.

She's a wannabe. One of the legions of them who wander the halls trying to copy Maggie Turner but don't quite pull it off. Never accepted by the It Girl, but never willing to give up their fascination with all things Maggie Turner, either. Lurking on the outside to take in every scrap of information. Anything that is even remotely connected to The Blondes makes them happy. Makes them feel closer to being on the inside.

That's why she wants to know about me.

She wants to know if I'm a new recruit. A potential It Girl. Someone worth talking to. Maybe it should bother me knowing it's the only reason Diana cares to get to know me. Lukas would think it should bother me. But somehow it doesn't. When you move around as much as I have, you take advantage of any way you can to make friends.

"I don't know," I tell her. "I haven't really thought about it."

Diana gasps like an actress in an old movie. So overly dramatic that I can't imagine that she's being anything but serious. "But you *have* to," she says. "It's not like they ask everybody." From her tone of voice, I can tell that *everybody* really means her, that they've never asked her to join.

"I guess, but it's not really my thing," I admit. "I've never seen myself as a cheerleader."

"But you'd be perfect!" Diana tells me. "Everyone's been saying you'd be perfect. I mean, all the prettiest girls end up on the squad eventually."

I slow down and stare at her. Something about the way she says it, as if there's nothing strange about it, gives me a chill. Almost the same thing Lukas has been saying to me, that they would try to make me one of them.

"Who's everybody?" I ask. The excited feeling that I had when we met a minute ago is replaced with a twisting inside my stomach like butterflies being squeezed to death.

Diana looks embarrassed for the first time. Blushing under her makeup and smiling nervously as if she let something slip that she wasn't supposed to. "The whole school," she says in a whisper. "Everybody could tell the first time they saw you. I mean, you're just as pretty as any of them," she says as we exit the school and step into the cold breeze blowing down from the hills on either side of town.

"Thanks," I mumble, not sure what else to say without sounding totally paranoid. Wondering if Diana is part of some great high-school conspiracy and knowing it would sound ridiculous if I ask. Besides, it's probably nothing. I'm probably just being stupid and she's probably just being nice.

I blame Lukas.

It's his fault for filling my head with all those warnings.

We take a few steps over the grass together before Diana tells me she's got to go the other way. Says good-bye but doesn't walk away. She waits for a second with the wind blowing against her face. "You know, you should really think about it," she tells me.

"Maybe I will," I say because it seems so important to her and for some reason I don't want to let her down. Not when we're just becoming friends.

It's the answer she wanted to hear. She smiles wider, facing the sun. Then she waves and hurries off in the other direction. I stand where I am for a minute and shake my head. No matter how many times I move, some things never change. Small towns being filled with strange people is certainly one of those things.

# FOUR

**My dad is used to seeing me mope around. I've gotten very** good at it over the last few years. He says so himself. Says I'm an expert. Which is why it surprises me that he can be so oblivious to the fact that I'm in a bad mood when he comes out of his bedroom Saturday morning and greets me with a smile.

The sun shining through the window blinds him as he takes a deep breath. "Isn't it a great day?" he asks me.

I roll my eyes at him and go back to blowing on my coffee. Watch the little ripples like waves traveling across a small pond. He doesn't notice, though, and goes right on talking about the wonders of this particular Saturday. Telling me how clean the air smells. Saying the wet scent of pine is like medicine.

"Dad, that's the smell of mold growing in this damp disgusting house," I tell him. "We'll probably both get sick from it."

"I see you're as bright and cheery as ever," he says, taking a mug from the cupboard. He doesn't say it in a mean way. He just thinks making jokes will snap me out of being grumpy. All it really does is get on my nerves.

"Whatever," I mumble and go back to staring out the window.

He pours himself a cup of coffee and takes yesterday's newspaper from the counter. Comes over to the table to join me. The chair scratching against the floor as he pulls it out. Sits down and reads the sulky expression on my face.

"Things still aren't going so well at school, huh?" he asks.

"Not exactly," I say. Saying it like an accusation. Saying it in a way that lets him know he's partially responsible because it was his idea to move here. Saying it mean enough to erase his smile.

I feel guilty about it right away.

I know it must be hard for him to raise me by himself and everything. I know he tries his best. That he has ever since my mom left us when I was just barely old enough to remember her. And I don't always make it easy for him. I can tell I'm not making it easy for him now, either. I can tell by the way he glances at me that he thinks he's letting me down.

"At least it's Saturday," is all he finally gets out.

It's not much of a comfort, but I give him a quick smile anyway the next time he looks at me. After all, it's not his fault that Morgan has picked me to be the target of her popularity poison ever since she heard that Meredith asked me to try out for the cheerleading squad. She's made me the subject of rumors about why I moved here. Rumors that get meaner as the days go on. Went from being a drug addict who dropped out to me being kicked out for having sex with a teacher. Those are just the ones I've heard about or have been written on notes shoved in my locker over the last few days. Whatever the other ones are, they're enough to keep me quarantined from the rest of the kids. Because I'm rubber and everyone else is glue and whatever the cheerleaders say about me sticks to them, too.

Everyone is too afraid to be seen with me. Meredith especially. Diana still talks to me but that's only because she's still hoping I'll finally make it. That somehow The Blondes will miraculously accept me and then she can be there to latch on to my newfound fame.

Lukas is the only one who doesn't seem to notice the rumors. Or he doesn't care, I should say. That's because no one else will talk to him, either. So he's more than happy to sit with me and share his theories about Maplecrest. Crazy ideas that he's taken straight out of the pages of all the horror comics he reads. The most pathetic part about it is that I'm actually glad for his company no matter how much I can't stand listening to them.

None of this will probably matter too long, anyway. My dad still hasn't found any work. And as I watch him go through the help-wanted ads, he doesn't seem to be circling many opportunities. If he doesn't find something soon, my problems might be solved before I know it.

"Any luck?" I ask, hoping to get an idea of just how soon I could be out of this place. Tucking my hands under my knees and crossing my fingers, hoping it will be sooner rather than later.

"I wouldn't call it luck," he says, folding the newspaper

over so he can look at me. "I did meet someone yesterday, though. Said he might be looking for part-time people," he tells me and my heart sinks a little.

I uncross my fingers and lift my hand up to my mouth. Lower my eyes to look at the table as I start to bite my nails. "Oh," I say. "I guess that means we're staying here."

My dad reaches across the table and puts his hand on my shoulder. He knows me well enough to know when I'm just being moody and when I'm really truly upset. "I'm afraid so. For a little bit, anyway," he says apologetically.

I shrug his hand away and push my chair back.

"Come on, Hannah," he says playfully. "It can't be that bad."

"Remember Buchanan?" I say, bringing up the middle school I went to for exactly two weeks. The two most embarrassing weeks of my life, thanks to puberty and my dad not knowing quite enough to teach me about the lifesaving properties of tampons. Two weeks of being called Hannah Bloody Hannah. And I can tell by the look that creeps across my dad's face that no matter how hard he's tried to forget, he still remembers it quite well. "It's almost as bad as that!" I say.

I see him hold back a smile and I know he thinks I'm exaggerating.

"Forget it! I knew you wouldn't understand," I say. I get up from my chair and storm off to my room. It's not fair that we get to pack up and leave when things don't work out for him. But when things don't work out for me, that's just too bad.

I hear him get up after I shut my door. I throw myself on my bed among the pile of clothes and homework and listen to the sound of his footsteps coming down the hall. I turn away when he opens the door. I don't want to see him. Don't want to talk to him. And if I could, I wouldn't hear him, either, when he says he's sorry.

"Just give it some time," he says. "Please. For me?"

"Time for what?" I say, speaking to his reflection standing in the window on the other side of my room. I know how cliques work. Giving it more time won't ever make them like me.

"I don't know. Maybe you'll meet some other kids," he says.

The houses across the street stare back at me from outside my window. Their rooms are all empty. Their lawns overgrown. FOR SALE signs flapping in the wind as leaves blow across the blacktop like tumbleweeds in a ghost town from old Westerns.

"What kids?" I ask him. His reflection floating behind the vacant windows of abandoned houses. "In case you haven't noticed, this town died a long time ago," I whisper. I'm talking more to myself than to him as I stare at the pink bag next to my head. "Now there's nothing left but cheerleaders and football players and the perfect little world they've made for themselves," I mumble. "And I don't fit into it," I say, tracing the shape of flowers on my backpack.

He doesn't say anything.

He just walks away.

That's fine with me. I like to be alone when I'm feeling sorry for myself, anyway.

**By the time** Lukas knocks on the door my dad has already left to see about that part-time job he mentioned. I watch him for a second through the peephole before answering. I wasn't expecting him to show up here. His shaggy brown hair being tossed around in the wind as he blows on his hands to get the autumn cold out and I debate whether I should open the door or let him shiver for as long as it takes before he decides to leave.

"Hannah?" he shouts, suddenly banging his fist against the door again.

I turn the knob and sigh.

"Oh, hey. I wasn't sure if you'd be here," he says. The anxious look I saw through the peephole is erased. Replaced with a polite smile. The shouting replaced with a softer volume. "Is it okay that I came by?" he asks.

I lean against the door frame with one hand on my hip and the other ready to shut him out. "What do you want, Lukas?" He's trying to sound annoyed, so he doesn't think he's saved me from my boredom. But being careful not to sound too annoyed because I don't want him to go away just yet.

He doesn't have any of the confidence that he pretends to have in the lunchroom. Not standing outside my house staring at me in my pajamas. Not when it shows all over his face that he likes me. Rosy cheeks that are a little too red to have been caused by the slight chill in the air. Brown eyes that won't look me in the eye, but can't keep themselves from looking at me.

"Um . . . ," he stutters. Shoves his hands in his jacket pockets and shifts his weight from one foot to the other. Taking his eyes off me for the first time and staring at his shoelaces instead. "I just thought I'd come by . . . see if you wanted to go to the game," he says.

The draft catches the corner of my shirt and lifts it above my waist. I grab it and pull it back down before Lukas looks up again. I scrunch up my face to let him know I have no idea what he's talking about.

"Our school's game," he says. "You know, the one all the stupid signs in the hallway are for?"

I know the signs. They went up all over school on Friday. Dumbest signs I've ever seen. Red with black letters scrawled in a scratchy handwriting. SUPPORT THE DEATH SQUAD! The lovely nickname the cheerleaders have given our football team. I guess our badger mascot wasn't tough enough.

"Why do you want to go there? I thought you hated everything about them?" I ask. Twisting the end of my hair around my finger and teasing him with a smile. Thinking I caught him in a lie. After the way he teased me for being curious about them, it turns out he may be just as curious.

"Yeah, I do," he says. "I just thought you might want to go. Then you could see what I've been trying to tell you all week."

"Yeah, right," I say. "I'm sure that's why."

Lukas sighs and tilts his head to the side. Watches the shapes in the clouds as they move in over the mountains in the distance and I can tell I'm making him frustrated. It's so easy with boys. At least with the ones who have a crush on me. And kind of fun, too. Especially with Lukas because he gets so animated. It's okay, though, it makes him cuter.

"Look, it's for your own good," he says.

I smile and tell him he sounds like my dad. Always telling me to go out, get some fresh air and it will be good for me.

"I'm serious," he says. "You'll see what I mean about everyone in this town being deranged." His hands clenched into tight fists as he pulls them from his pockets. His eyes pleading. Begging me almost.

"Oh, I forgot," I say, trying my best not to laugh as I remember some of the crazy things he told me when he was finally willing to let me in on the town's *dangerous* secret. "What was it again? They're all vampires or something?" I ask, giggling as I think about the expression on his face when he told me. Remembering how serious he looked and how surprised he was when I laughed.

"Not vampires—zombies!" he says and I don't try to hold it in anymore. I start laughing like a little kid. The redness in his cheeks stays, but it's more from anger than anything else now. "Laugh if you want, but it's true. I'll show you," he says, more frustrated than before.

"I think you've read one too many of those stupid comics," I tell him.

I think I hurt his feelings with that one because he sighs and shakes his head. Looks at me slightly in the same way I've seen him look at Maggie and her clones as if to tell me I'm just like them. Just like everyone else who won't listen to him.

"Just forget it," he says and starts to walk off my front step.

"I didn't say I wouldn't go with you," I call out as he gets to the driveway. Putting my hands on my hips like I'm challenging him. Testing him to see how much he really likes me by seeing how much he'll put up with. And apparently he likes me enough to turn around because he starts walking back up to the door. "I'll go," I say. It can't be worse than sitting in here all day and watching terrible movies on television. "Just let me get dressed, okay?" I say and he nods.

I open the door wider and invite him to wait inside. He steps in and I head toward my bedroom. Glancing back to see if he's looking at the lack of furniture in our house and if it changes his mind about me. But he doesn't seem to notice. Just sits down and waits and I realize I could do a lot worse than to have a friend like him.

"Just so you know, this isn't a date," I yell out before disappearing into my room. More of a joke than anything else. I just don't want him getting too comfortable, that's all.

Who are all those people?" I ask. I didn't expect to see so many people in attendance, not nearly as many as I see when we trample across the grass separating the sidewalk from the football field. The crowd fills both sets of bleachers and spills over onto the lawn. On the grass, people are lined up two and three deep, clinging to the fence that circles the field. Surging forward to get the best view. Politely shoving and pushing their way to the front.

"It's all of Maplecrest," Lukas says without any sort of

expression. Says it's not an exaggeration, either. That the whole town turns out for home games.

"Why?" I ask. Holding on to his sleeve as we make our way through the crowd, knowing that if I let go I'll be swallowed by the sea of strangers and never find him again. "I mean, I know there's not much to do here . . . but still?"

"I told you why," Lukas says. Fighting forward by swinging his elbows and no one really seems to mind getting nudged or even notices that much. "It's like they're all brainwashed," he tells me. Points with his thumb at no one in particular. Pointing at the crowd in general.

I notice the glazed look in everyone's eyes. The way pupils are all large enough for me to see the clouds change with the wind. The anticipation of violence making hands tremble. Speaking to each other only in hushed phrases and never taking eyes away from the action that has yet to start.

I wouldn't go so far as to call it brainwashed, but I have to admit it weirds me out a little the way we're invisible as we shuffle through.

"Come on! We'll go all the way to the top. No one ever sits that far back," he says, leading me up to the bleachers as I see the opposing team take the field. I listen for any sign of applause for them as we climb the steps but they're only greeted with silence and a scattering of boos. I pause to look around, wondering why no one from their town is here. Not even parents. Not any who are willing to show support, anyway.

I ask Lukas about it as we reach the top row and sit down. My words escaping between the rise and fall of my chest as I try to catch my breath. He tells me they never come. Says it's too long of a drive because all the schools we play are from far away. That none of the schools nearby will play us anymore. Too many kids getting hurt. "That's how they came up with the stupid Death Squad stuff," he says.

I roll my eyes. I find the whole thing nauseating.

I'm beginning to wonder why I came in the first place just as the whispers from the crowd die down. Fade out. And a silence takes over like every breath of air has been stolen from each set of lungs in attendance as everyone watches a parade of paper-thin blondes dressed in black uniforms strut onto the field.

A deafening roar erupts once the cheerleaders have assembled in the middle of the grass. The noise fills the valley and makes the last of the leaves cling for life on the branches of nearby trees. A faint glow shows in the faces of the people sitting around us when they get a glimpse of the girls in their short skirts. Pale like angels and eyes the color of heaven. Casting a spell on the town and even the clouds break apart. The afternoon sun breaks through and shines like a halo above their golden heads.

The calls from the crowd stop as suddenly as they started. Trailing off to a whisper again before falling silent as Maggie raises one fist in the air. Demanding the full attention of every pair of glassy eyes and each obeys. Focusing solely on the bend of her elbow and angle of her wrist.

"See what I mean?" Lukas whispers in my ear. "This place is like a cult, and she's their leader," he says, pointing at Maggie. He keeps whispering as they begin their routine. Mumbling more of his conspiracy theories as the other girls move in close to Maggie and lift her up. Tells me how Maggie makes them all change their names so that they start with the same letter. Says once a girl gets on the squad, she has to dye her hair. Has to become a clone like Morgan. Like Meredith. Like all the rest of them who are helping toss Maggie into the air. "And the rest of the town goes along with it," he says. Making sure I know that he means the rest of the town minus him.

And as much as I want to agree with him, as much as I want to hate all of them for Morgan's nasty looks and name-calling, I can't help but be as fascinated as everyone else when Maggie soars higher and higher. Tucking her legs into her chest and tumbling three or four times before twisting around and landing perfectly on the ground.

"How does she do that?" I ask in amazement. It doesn't seem possible. She seems too frail with her bones showing through under her skin. Too thin to have the strength or energy.

"She's undead, that's how," Lukas says, deadly serious.

I ignore him and keep watching the routine as the girls form a tight circle so that from any angle, it looks like there's only one of them. When they can't get any closer together, the marching band begins to play. With each beat, they move farther apart. The girl in the center multiplying. Identical twins sprouting on each side. And I finally understand why they need to look alike. Makes it more theatrical. More mes-merizing. It actually looks cool in a spooky sort of way.

A wave of quiet sweeps over the bleachers when Maggie raises her hand into the air once more. A tingling feeling rushes along my skin like someone scratching on glass or steel scraping across blacktop.

The clean smiles on their faces disappear. Their eyes open wide and fearful and the crowd mirrors them. Follows them with their eyes as they march stiffly to the sound of the drums. Forming letters on the field as the people shout them in rhythm.

"D-

"E-

"A-

"T-

"H-

"DEATH!

"DEATH!

"DEATH!"

The chant shouted at the top of their lungs. Stomping their feet to the cadence. The bleachers trembling from the volume and vibration. Everyone's face as pale and blank as those on the field. Mouths moving mechanically. Threateningly. The chant raining down onto the field like a violent storm that makes the opposing team cringe.

"Still think I'm crazy?" Lukas whispers.

The people around us wake up from their trance. Blink their eyes and start to strike up conversations. Slowly returning to normal as the cheerleaders break formation.

"Okay, it's pretty strange," I admit.

"Pretty strange?" Lukas says in disbelief. "It's a freak show!"

The girl next to him stares with suspicious eyes when he yells. Whispers something to the girl she's with. Lukas turns to her with the face of a snarling animal and she slides away a few inches.

"What's your problem?" I whisper. Grab his sleeve and pull him closer like calling off an attack dog.

"My problem's that we're about to watch those kids get torn apart by vicious flesh-eating creatures and this whole town can't wait to see it," he says. He's careful to be quiet enough so no one else hears. Keeps glancing around just to make sure.

"Now the football team is part of it, too?" I tease.

"Of course they're part of it!" he says. "Haven't you noticed they're all just as pale? Their eyes just as blue? Just as dead?"

I guess I hadn't paid too much attention to them. All jocks look the same to me, anyway. And most of the ones I've met are vicious and brutal, so since the ones in Maplecrest are especially violent, it only means they're good at what they've been trained to do. "Seriously, Lukas, you need to cut down on the comic books," I tell him. At first I thought he was just making it up. Trying to get me to pretend along with him so it would be like me and him against all of them. I thought it was kind of cute. Sort of sweet and everything, but now I'm starting to think he actually believes it.

"Whatever," he says and stops talking to me. Leans back against the railing behind us. Tilts his head up to the sky as the game begins. Fine with me. This town is bad enough without him trying to convince me that it's home to an army of beautiful walking-dead elitists.

He keeps sulking behind me. Blowing his breath out and sighing.

I do my best to ignore him. Refuse to look over my

shoulder and get his attention or listen to any more of his horror stories.

I watch the teams on the field instead and have no idea what's going on.

I've never understood football. It's always just seemed like a bunch of guys jumping on one another and grunting. My dad tried to explain it to me once. He said it was simple. Then he went on and on about different rules and exceptions, and after about five minutes it didn't sound so simple anymore so I told him to stop. If it was that complicated, I didn't want to waste space in my brain learning about it.

But I don't have to understand it to know our team is winning.

I can tell by the way our players swarm at whoever has the ball. Twisting his body to the sound of cracking bones. The agony in the screams as the other players lie mangled on the field. The chilling shouts from the crowd as they cheer and I realize the Death chant wasn't just for show. The players from our side are really trying their best to kill the opposition.

But that's how the game is played, isn't it? It doesn't mean they're zombies or anything like that. Doesn't mean they really want to tear off their helmets and rip through their flesh with hungry teeth. Just means they want to win worse than anything else. It just means they're jocks, that's all. Still, though, there is something eerie about the whole thing. About the whole town in general. Not just the game or that it's like the last fifty years have missed this place completely. It's also the way no one can take their eyes off the cheerleaders whenever they step onto the field. Vacant and hypnotized because the violence around them has a way of making them look even more beautiful. Even more like angels. Like snowflakes falling over a battlefield.

"Seen enough?" Lukas asks when the game reaches halftime.

"Yeah," I mumble. "Let's go."

And as we head down the steps, I find that I can't take my eyes off them, either. Wondering what it must be like to have people look at you that way. Wondering what it would be like to have that much control over total strangers.

"Wait," I say softly, holding on to Lukas. Pausing at the bottom of the bleachers as Maggie leads the girls onto the field again. The cold breeze washing over all of us. Stealing the color from their cheeks and bringing it to me. "I just want to see this before we leave."

# FIVE

**Whenever my dad and I take one of our long drives to a new**
life, I like to stare out the window and watch normal people
doing normal things in each town we pass. I always see kids
doing things that I know are pretty common, but that seem
so distant to me. Bake sales and car-wash fund-raisers. Signs
in front of schools for class plays. Even large groups of friends
just walking together down the sidewalk seems like something I could never be a part of.

I'm always the one left out.

If high school were like little kids on the playground, I'd
be the little kid sitting on the swings all by herself. That's
who I am. Always the girl who doesn't quite fit in. It's not
because I'm weird or because I want to be an outsider. It's
just that being the kid who moves to town, I've always missed
the start of the game and by the time I get there, they don't
need anyone else to play.

I guess that's why I haven't been able to get the cheer-leading routine out of my head. Since the football game yesterday, it's all I can think about. Something about it is so amazing. So perfect. Just like those scenes of normal people that pass by the car window.

And I keep thinking about Meredith asking me if I've ever thought about joining. And I think maybe I might. I know it's sort of dumb. But just once I'd like to see what it would be like to be one of the group instead of being the kid alone on the swings.

"What are you thinking about, Squirt?"

My dad's voice pulls me out of my daytime-television fog long enough to wrinkle my forehead at him. "Dad, I stopped being Squirt years ago," I tell him. "Can't you find a nickname that's not so dumb?"

He smiles as he sits down next to me on the sofa. Tells me no matter how big I get, I'll always be his *Squirt* and I roll my eyes.

"Perfect," I say. "At least now I know that I'll be uncool forever."

He ignores my comeback as usual and takes the remote from my knee. The television doesn't respond to the buttons his fingers push, though. He adjusts the tape that wraps around the remote to hold in the batteries. Taps it gently against the palm of his hand before aiming again. Still no response and his tapping turns into a more violent banging.

"This thing's busted," he mumbles.

"No, it just doesn't like your shows," I say. I reach over and take it back from him. Press the same buttons he did and the channel changes as easily as that. "See, it just needs a girl's touch."

"Thanks," he says. Then he puts his arm around me and I know he's thanking me for more than just fixing the remote. I know he's thanking me for just being there. For being me.

It's the little things like this that he was talking about when he called us a team. The same things that can almost make me forget about trying to be popular or fitting in. I can forget that we're not normal. I can almost convince myself that we're better than those people who live in big houses and have three cars and buy whatever they want. When we sit on a torn-up sofa that was left in the house and watch bad television, I can almost convince myself that everything is perfect.

Almost.

Because then something always happens that reminds me our life kind of sucks.

"Oh," my dad says, acting like he just remembered something but doing a bad job of it. "If the phone rings, don't answer it."

I sit up straight. Putting my hands on my knees and staring at him.

"Why?" I demand.

My dad shrugs it off. "It's nothing." His standard answer.

I shake my head and stand up. He asks me where I'm going. Asks why I'm leaving. "Because," I tell him and that's all I tell him. Because he knows why. Because he knows what *because* means. It means I know why we're not answering the phone. I know it means someone found us. Someone he owes money to. They always find us because running away never works.

No wonder I'm always the outcast. I live in a house where we can't even answer the phone!

I don't listen as he calls for me to come back. I head right to my room and close the door. I'm not in the mood to hear his explanations. I don't need to listen to his speech about how everything will be just fine one day. I already have it memorized.

Lying on my bed, I stare out the window and try to think of something else. Anything else. And the blue sky brings me back to them. The clear eyes of the girls everybody in Maplecrest loves. And maybe it's not such a bad idea after all to be like them. Maybe becoming a clone of Maggie Turner wouldn't be as horrible as it sounded on my first day of school. At least being somebody else for a while would take my mind off of being me. It would get Morgan off my case, too. And to tell the truth, I wouldn't mind being adored for once in my life.

I know it's probably crazy, but it's pretty to think of, in that way.

# SIX

You're going to what?" Lukas says over the steady chatter of the lunchroom. Pushing his chair away and letting his fists fall on the table. Two girls at the next table stop eating. They stare at us for a second trying to figure out who's shouting. Turn around again when they see us because we're not important enough for them to care.

"You're making a scene," I whisper.

"Sorry," he says sarcastically. "I wouldn't want to embarrass you in front of your new friends." Still speaking loud enough to make the next table glance over. Trying to say it loud enough to get Maggie and her group to look over from their table but it's too far away for his voice to travel. Too much static between here and there.

"Don't be a jerk," I say seriously enough to let him know I'm only half kidding.

"I'm being a jerk?" he asks. An honest show of confusion

on his face when he raises his eyebrows and lets his shaggy hair fall in front of his eyes. Then he gathers himself. Takes a deep breath and takes my wrists in his hands. I look down real quick, surprised by how warm his skin feels. Surprised by how familiar it feels. "Hannah, listen to yourself. I'm being a jerk? They wrote SLUTS NOT WELCOME on your locker last Friday, remember?" he says, nodding over to the table of power that rules our little high school society.

I pull my hands away violently.

"I don't need you to remind me," I say. "I still see it every time I need a book. Besides, it wasn't all of them. It was just Morgan."

"Oh, that makes a difference," he says.

"It does," I snap at him.

"I can't believe you're talking about trying out for the cheerleading squad. It's enemy territory," he says, throwing his arms up in the air as if he's proven his point.

I don't say anything.

The truth is, I'm not sure he isn't right about it. Maybe it is a crazy idea. Maybe he's right to talk me out of it. I know he's just trying to look out for me. Doesn't want to see me get my feelings hurt. But I haven't been able to stop thinking about the way the girls looked ever since we saw them at the game two days ago. The way the crowd couldn't take their eyes away for fear they might miss even a second of the routine. And I guess I just want that, too. Want people to look at me that way. Even if it's only in this lost little town in the middle of nowhere. Even if it's just once.

Lukas brushes the hair away from his face. Pulls his chair closer to me. His brown eyes look safe against the red and black walls in the background. "Don't you see? That's what they do," he says in a quieter voice. A friendlier one. "They make it so girls want to become one of them. Then once you do, that's it. You're not Hannah anymore. You're Mara. Or Monica. Or whatever name she gives you."

"I just want to try out, not become someone else," I tell him. Sort of telling myself at the same time because I'd be lying if it didn't cross my mind.

"That's what Alison said," he says. His eyes go someplace far away. Looking over the heads of all the seated people in the room. Staring like if he stares long enough, hard enough, he'll be able to see into the past.

"Who's Alison?" I ask.

Lukas shakes off the memories that are like movie images playing against the back of his eyelids. "Alison is Morgan," he says. "She used to be a good friend of mine. Now she doesn't even remember who I am."

"Morgan?" I say, surprised that he'd ever be friends with such a superior bitch. "You're better off."

"But that's what I'm trying to tell you, she didn't used to be like that," he says. Raising his voice again the way my dad does when he's lost patience with me. I'm about to tell him he's leaning toward being a jerk again when he says he's sorry. Lowers his voice. "It's just . . . I get upset when I think about it . . . like I should've stopped her or something."

"Look, it's no big deal. It's just something to do," I say. Trying to comfort him. To assure him that the same thing won't happen with me. I didn't mean to upset him. I mean, I guess I knew he wouldn't be happy about it, but I didn't think he'd get all freaked out about it. "Besides, don't you watch the news? Self-esteem is very important for a girl my age. It could mean the difference between being president and being a prostitute," trying to make a joke out of the whole thing so that he sees I'm not too serious about it.

"I knew this would happen," he says. "I knew it as soon as I saw you the first time. That's why I came over in the first place. To warn you off."

"Don't you think you're overreacting?" I say. "I mean, they're cheerleaders, not terrorists."

"You don't get it," he says. "They're already dead. They only walk and breathe because they feed off the living."

"Not this again!" It's my turn to raise my voice. "I've had it with all this crap. You need to come back to the real world," I tell him. Because I'm beginning to think he's the one who needs to be saved.

"Hannah, why do you think there're so many empty houses in this town? Why do you think the whole school is terrified of them? It's not just because they're popular and mean. It's because they kill people. Kill them and use their blood to keep their corpses from rotting!" He's talking so fast and so whispered that his face gets flushed.

"Yeah? Then how come they don't kill you? If you know so much, wouldn't they want to?" I ask.

"Everybody knows! Don't you get it?" he growls, trying to keep his voice from being heard but also trying to sound fierce. "Only nobody talks about it. Not even me . . . not to anybody but you."

"Oh, lucky me," I say sarcastically and shuffle my books and chair to inch away from him.

Lukas moves his chair, too. Moves closer. Cupping his hand around my ear and whispering so that his words are warm and wet. "They're going to make you like that," he says. "They're going to make it so you have to kill, too."

I push him away and put my hands up to my ears to let him know how ridiculous he sounds. His eyes are crazy. Eyes like angry dogs barking behind fences to keep people out. Eyes like the kind of people he's trying to warn me against.

He reaches over and pulls my hand away.

I'm no longer playing when I struggle free. "Get off of me!" I tell him.

"Look at them!" he says, keeping his fingers wrapped around my wrist as I try to pull away. "Look in their eyes. They're not like us."

"You're crazy," I tell him once I finally peel his hands off my arm. Little white marks still there to outline where he held on. "Nobody's killing anybody! This town's empty because it sucks. There's nothing to do and no place to work. That's why people move, not because they're being stalked by imaginary creatures. And that's why I'm going to try out . . . because I'm bored!"

All the faces at the tables on both sides are turned to face us when I'm done shouting. The teacher's aide assigned to the lunchroom is staring at us from across the room. Watching as I rub my arm and wondering if she needs to get involved. I hear the girls next to me whispering. "Jesus! He's such a freak," they say. Lukas hears them, too, but doesn't let it break his concentration. Doesn't take his eyes from mine. Stares so intensely that it scares me.

I'm not sure what to do as I see the corners of his eyes get bloodshot. See them blur up and I know I've hurt him pretty bad. I didn't mean to. Not after he's been the only person nice enough to get to know me. But there's a reason no one talks to him. Maybe he really is a freak. I didn't think so, but I'm starting to wonder because I know now that he honestly believes what he's telling me.

"Forget it," he says. "All of it, it doesn't matter. Try out and have fun. I hope you make it. At least then I'll never have to see you again."

He grabs his backpack off the floor and stands up.

"Lukas! Wait!" I plead.

But he doesn't stop and I watch him fade into the crowd. Watch my only friend in Maplecrest disappear from my life. I fold my arms on the table and hide my head in the crease of my elbow, wondering why every boy I ever meet turns out to be a creep.

I won't let him change my mind, though. I'm going to see the cheerleading coach as soon as lunch is over. It's the only way I'll ever be able to make any sane friends here.

I'll show him, too. I won't change even if I do make the squad. Maybe then he'll realize how insane he's being.

**Have you ever** cheered before?" Mrs. Donner asks me as I stand in front of her desk, shuffling my feet and looking for the proper place to put my hands. I stick them in my pockets but they feel uncomfortably tight and so I pull them out again. Hide them behind my back and twist the fingers of my left hand with the fingers of my right hand the same way my dad showed me to do with paper before making a fire in the fireplace and give myself small Indian burns as I think about the question of having ever cheered before.

"Not exactly," is the answer I settle on.

Mrs. Donner lets her glasses slide down to the end of her nose and looks at me from above the lenses. Her eyes are like blue sparks of electricity bursting under an icy surface. If it wasn't for their sharp color, there would be nothing about this lady that would connect her to the girls she coaches on the cheerleading squad. She has none of their perfection. Her face is lined with age and her skin has taken on the gray color of ashes that old people often get. Her dress is drab and shapeless and makes her look like a giant hen sitting on her roost. But the eyes are the same and I wonder if she was pale and thin and beautiful once, too.

"You know we have a very high standard," she tells me in a flat tone.

I nod. Thinking about my own beauty and wondering if she's saying that as a way of letting me know I'm also far from being flawless.

She covers her mouth with the palm of her hand and taps her fingers against her cheek. The glare of the sun catches her glasses and erases her eyes. Two blank circles stare at me and I start to feel self-conscious as she tilts her head to one side and then the other trying to get a good look at every part of me. Then she asks me again if I've ever had any experience.

I bite my lip and consider lying to her and telling her that I used to cheer. It wouldn't be a complete lie. I used to cheer when I was seven years old. I'd twirl around and wave my pom-poms out of rhythm to the chant and pretend I was a ballerina when my skirt lifted into the air. But I know that's not what she means and she'd be able to see through it. Her eyes are the kind that can pull the truth out like a magnet. So I keep my response vague like before.

"Sort of," I say, putting my hands back in my pockets.

A skeptical look transforms her face and I can tell right away it's not going to be enough.

"Well, I did do gymnastics for two years," saying it a little too quickly, a little too eagerly. It's the truth, though. I just leave out the part about it having been over a year since I've practiced anything.

"Gymnastics?" Mrs. Donner says and smiles patiently the way people do when they're listening to little kids tell a story that doesn't make any sense.

"I know it's not the same thing," I admit, "but some of it is. I can learn the rest of it if you give me the chance." The chance is all I want. All I'm asking for and nothing more. One try to show everyone I'm not what I've been made out to be through whispers slipping off slithering tongues.

The tap-tapping of her fingers drumming against her chin starts over again and I start to sway at the hips. I can hear voices drifting in from the hallway as the minute hand ticks closer to class time. My stomach begins to turn over and over as Mrs. Donner considers me. Taking my hand from my pocket, I start to bite my nails. She catches me and gives a stern look. The kind of look teachers give to address any bad habit and I take my hand away from my mouth. It's clear that nail biting certainly doesn't go along with her high standard.

Mrs. Donner seems happy that I've caught on so quickly. She smiles and the wrinkles disappear to wipe the age away from her face. "Okay, let's see what you can do," she finally says and I feel the knots inside me begin to loosen.

"Thank you!" I shout, bringing my hands together as if saying a prayer. My heart races inside me like a bird beating its wings against the bars of a cage and I can't stop smiling. "I won't let you down," I promise her and she nods to show she doesn't expect me to.

"See you after school, then," she says with a reminder of where and when I'm supposed to report to face my fate. I nod and hurry past the kids who are filing into the room. Wave once over my shoulder as my reflection grows smaller in the glare of her eyeglasses.

The hall is a dizzy maze of backpacks and blue jeans and colored lockers and dust specks that catch in the sunlight. Same as it was this morning, but somehow it looks different. Brighter. And the faces going by don't look nearly as threatening because already something has changed. Already I'm starting over and this time whatever I become here it will be because of things I choose to do instead of stories made up about me.

I'm so lost in my thoughts that I don't notice the person hurrying behind me. Not until she grabs the strap of my backpack. The surprise of it makes me gasp and stumble until I see it's only Diana.

"I saw you talking to Mrs. Donner," she says. She looks as excited about it as I do. Maybe even more excited. "Does that mean you're thinking about joining the squad?" she asks.

"Yeah, I'm supposed to try out after school today," I tell her and my new identity is secured by the expression on her face. I'm no longer the strange girl with rumors swirling over my head. I'm now someone who might actually be somebody and I can't help but smile at her.

"Wow! I can't believe she's really letting you try out," Diana says, matching my pace as we walk to our next class together. "She doesn't usually let anyone try out after the first two weeks of school."

"I guess I'm lucky," I say, shrugging my shoulders, wondering why Mrs. Donner would break her own rules for me. Feeling slightly proud about it. About being an exception. Being special in the eyes of someone who values perfection.

"You're gonna make it, I just know it," Diana says.

"Thanks," I say, wishing I were as confident as she is. I put my head down as we walk to hide how unsure I am. I don't know why, but I feel like it would let her down if she saw.

Diana stops me again right before we're about to go in. She waits until I'm looking at her, until she knows I'm paying attention. "One last thing," she says, glancing around as the hallways clear out and making sure no one is listening. "Don't worry if the other girls give you a hard time. It's just a test to see if you're really cut out for it. It's the way it always happens—you'll do fine," she tells me.

A laundry list of nasty lies about me scrolls across her eyes and it's my turn to blush a little knowing she's heard every one of the things Morgan has said about me. But they don't mean anything to her. I can tell by the way she smiles at me.

I want to ask her if she knows anything else, any tricks

that might help me during my trial, but our teacher steps out into the hallway and clears her throat.

"Diana, you're late," she says with a hatred that seems too strong for the situation. The kind that teachers reserve for students that they've built up a dislike for over a period of time. Even having just met her, I'm not so surprised. I've already gathered that Diana likes to talk a lot, a habit that probably doesn't stop just because class starts.

"I'm sorry," Diana says softly and lowers her head as she walks past the slouching figure in the doorway. Once she's inside, she glances over her shoulder and gives me a little wink. The kind that friends give each other.

"You're late, too," our teacher says, looking at me for the first time. Her voice not nearly as angry, but not exactly pleasant, either. I apologize and explain that I had to see Mrs. Donner about something.

My teacher's sour expression changes at the mention of Mrs. Donner's name. She's tells me not to worry about it, to consider it a warning. It's my first taste of the privileges granted to all The Blondes of Maplecrest High and I have to admit I could get used to it, no matter how strange the whole thing is.

# SEVEN

It happened when my dad and I were still living in the city.
When I was in third grade and my dad was still a cop. Jason,
a boy in my class with one lazy eye and no friends at all, sat
behind me. He always had a runny nose that he wiped on
his sleeve instead of using a tissue. I can remember being
terrified every time I heard him sniffle. I was always worried
that he'd somehow get snot all over the back of my chair
and it used to make me squirm. So one time when he
started his disgusting routine of snorting and sniveling, I
turned around and wrinkled up my nose at him to let him
know he was the grossest creature on the face of the earth.

We were enemies ever after and he developed more and
more disgusting noises to go along with the ones that already upset me. Purposely exaggerating them to get on my
nerves and giggling when it caused me to squirm. There was
definitely something not right with him and I remember

thinking he belonged in the special class at the end of the hall. His eyes always had a faint yellow glow to them like cats' eyes whenever he looked at me. Planning. Scheming. Waiting for the moment to strike until the time was right.

During one particular outburst of sneezing, I swore I felt a drop of something wet and slimy touch the back of my neck. I screamed. Yelled out to the teacher without raising my hand that Jason had spread his germs to me. Our other classmates felt the same way about him as I did and took my side, erupting in laughter and forever giving Jason the nickname of Germ Boy.

The next day, he struck back.

There was no warning. No series of sniffling or sneezes or snotty throat clearing. He struck in silence. Only the feel of his fingers combing through my hair with a sticky substance that made me freeze. By the time I turned around in my seat, the damage was done.

My hair didn't turn with the rest of me. It was stuck to his dirt-stained fingers with something more horrifying than snot. A pink web of chewing gum stretched from his palm to the clumped strands of my curly hair. The streaks of gum growing thinner as he pulled farther until they snapped, dangling like pink plastic hair weaved into my own.

The horrified faces of my friends confirmed my worst fears as I put my hand up to gauge how bad it really was. All the twisting and fighting I'd done had made it worse and left me with knotted tangles of stiff hair like the twigs of a bird's nest.

I didn't cry until I saw the first snip of my hair falling to the floor in the nurse's office as she closed the scissors effort-lessly in her crooked hand. That's when I cried. The tears running down my face with each clipping until I thought I'd run out of hair for her to cut because the floor was lit-tered with clumps that looked like furry kittens scattered for a nap.

When I finally saw my reflection in the medicine cabinet, I was as ugly as a boy.

I refused to go back to class. I made the nurse call my dad and made him leave work to come pick me up. He did his best to smile when he saw me. Ruffled my hair and told me I was still the prettiest girl in Brooklyn but I could tell by the angry sneer he gave the school nurse that he was as pissed as I was that she hadn't let a professional hairstylist handle the operation. And I could tell he also wanted to squeeze his hands around Jason's neck so tightly that his yel-low eyes popped out of his head and all the snot oozed out of his sockets.

I'm not sure why this is the story that pops into my head as I lie on the ground with my eyes closed. Not sure if it's because I want my dad to come ruffle my hair and tell me it'll all be all right or if it's just because I feel the same way I did then. Never wanting to face anyone again. I stayed home from school for a week after that. I didn't want to leave the house because everyone would think I was a boy. I wore dresses and ribbons for a month until my hair grew out. And as bad as it was, at least there was a way around it. I don't see my present situation having any such easy solutions.

"Someone help her up," Mrs. Donner's creaky voice says through the fog that clouds my thoughts.

I hear other voices, too. Closer ones. Kneeling beside me. Slithering voices of the girls whose arms I last saw stretched across the ground to catch me, only to break apart at the last second.

The palm of one hand closes on the back of my head as I lie facedown. Applying pressure and pushing my face gently until I taste dirt in my mouth. "Better watch yourself," a voice sneers in my ear, Morgan's voice, and I can feel her breath against my skin. Warm and angry like a dog with sharp teeth that just wants to growl but letting you know it can bite at any time. "Next time you might find yourself underground instead of on top of it," she says, smooshing my face harder like she's trying to bury me alive.

"Give her room. Step aside," Mrs. Donner says, getting nearer as I sense the crowding bodies hovering above me starting to move away.

The throbbing starts the second I open my eyes and see stars in the grass. Green stars smeared with the clear vomit dripping from my chin. I wipe it away with the sleeve of my sweatshirt just like Jason with his nose and the perfect angels of Maplecrest look at me the same way I looked at him.

"Are you okay?" the two whitewashed circles of Mrs. Donner's glasses ask me as I blink to get used to the glare of the afternoon sun. The wind is knocked out of me and I cough for air and nod unconvincingly that I'm fine. But she's already turned her attention to Miranda standing nearby with a hand covering her mouth to hide that she's giggling along with the other girl who was supposed to catch me. "I'm not laughing," Mrs. Donner tells them through clenched teeth and they stop immediately.

The clouds move across the sun and cast a shadow over Miranda as she stands up straighter. "I'm sorry," she says innocently. "I wasn't ready. I thought she was going to flip once more."

She tilts her head sympathetically toward me and a sugar-and-spice smile parts her lips. But her eyes look hungry, shining through the shadows. The pink skin around them itching with an evil glow. And not just her, but all of them. Standing over me in a circle like vultures waiting to pick my bones. Standing perfectly still with mischievous grins like the ghouls drawn in the pages of Lukas's comics.

I get up quickly and brush the dirt from my knees. Blow on my palms streaked with thin red lines of blood from pebble scrapes. The sight of my blood and the grass stains streaked across my face causes Miranda to lick her lips with satisfaction at my defeat.

"My bad," she says coldly and the rest of the girls laugh.

Mrs. Donner rests her hand between my shoulder blades and says, "I think that will be enough." Tells me she'll let me know even though it's clear that I not only didn't make the squad but took a giant step backward in my social life at the same time, despite that it's nearly impossible to sink lower in the ranks than I already am. "You sure you're okay? Do you want to go to the nurse to be sure?" she asks.

I shake my head.

Visions of gum-strewn hair and sharp scissors flash before me.

"Okay, but Morgan will go with you to make sure you're

all right," and she gestures for Morgan to help me back to the locker room.

Morgan looks as unhappy about it as I do and we both protest, but Mrs. Donner doesn't listen. Raises her hand to silence us and sends us on our way by clapping her hands to resume practice and orders the remaining girls to get into formation.

"Well, let's go, loser," Morgan groans, throwing her arms out impatiently before turning around and marching off toward the school building. I follow a good five or six steps behind, not wanting to be anywhere near her. Not wanting to hear her ridicule me with a play-by-play of everything I did wrong during the tryout. Wanting only to become invisible so that I never have to face the humiliation that I know is waiting for me day in and day out.

If I stayed home for a week in third grade because my hair was chopped off, I wonder how long I'll need to avoid school after this. Falling twelve feet to the ground and vomiting on impact in front of the girls who have the power to embarrass me with it forever? That should be good for a year off. A few months at the very least.

I should have listened to Lukas after all. I should have stayed away. It was an idiotic idea. But I guess it's always easier to say that after I've made a huge mistake. It always seems so simple afterward. By then there's nothing left to do but give in to the swollen feeling in the back of my throat and let the tears run quietly down my face.

I'm glad the lights haven't yet come on inside the locker room. The autumn sun has already dipped below the hills and only the softest orange glow seeps in from the small windows near the ceiling. In the dim light, Morgan can't see me feeling sorry for myself. Even if she can sense it, even if she does try to rub it in, at least I can take comfort knowing she can't actually see how much it hurts.

"I can't believe you even dared to try out," she says from the far corner of the room as I open the locker and take my things out. I can see her out of the corner of my eye, leaning against the wall with her arms crossed and her head tilted back. One leg bent at the knee and one foot resting against the cinder blocks. Acting as superior as she can and I can't stand her and everyone like her.

"I can't believe Lukas said you used to be nice," I mumble as I pull my hair into a wool hat to hide the sick matting it down.

Morgan pushes herself away from the wall and sprints toward me. I brace myself thinking for a second she's going to attack me, but she stops a few inches in front of me with her hands squeezed so tightly that the blood rushes out and leaves her fingers as white as the bleached tiles in the showers lining the wall behind her.

"Your freak boyfriend doesn't know anything," she says. Her eyes, fierce like a tiger's, wanting to rip me into little pieces.

"He's not my boyfriend . . . Alison," I sneer, no longer afraid to stand up to her because I no longer have anything to lose. No need to play it safe anymore because they already hate me. No chance of that changing. Not now. So I might as well play as mean as they do.

"Alison is dead," Morgan barks. Something dangerous in her words. In the way she shows her teeth when she leans closer to me. Her hands slowly coming up like she's going to strangle me and I can't even bring myself to scream. "You might even get to meet her soon enough," she threatens and my legs unlock as I stumble backward, falling over the bench behind me and landing with my head clanging against the metal lockers.

I reach my hand up to the back of my head and mouth a silent sound of pain that is drowned out by Morgan snickering behind her closed smile.

I don't move. Stay on the ground and play like a wounded animal as she steps over me. Prancing away like a cat having finished playing with a caught mouse even though it's only half killed. The sound of her laughter echoing off the locker room walls and mixing with the rattling of metal doors as she drags her hand against the lockers when she walks.

"I'm not afraid of you," I mumble. "Diana told me you were just full of talk," exaggerating what Diana really said. Morgan's eyes flash like dynamite and I worry that I accidentally brought Diana into the mess I've made.

"That stupid girl was wrong," Morgan says, shaking her head. "You'll see."

She pauses in front of the equipment room door and lets her fingernails scratch its surface. A piercing screech like the sharpening of knives rings out as her hand slides down. Her fingers wrap around the padlock hanging from the door's handle and plays with it for a second before turning around as if she forgot something. Drops the lock and lets it bang against the door with a wide smile. A stray ray of sun strikes her eyes and they flash like fireworks in the night sky.

"See you in school tomorrow," she says before opening the exit door and vanishing into the last breath of daylight.

I let the evening air wrap around me, wearing the cold like a protective blanket that keeps me numb to all the broken promises that come off my father's tongue and drop to the driveway like poison snow.

"It won't be for long," he says. "Maybe ten days. Two weeks tops."

The straps slide through my fingers and my bag falls to the concrete as he loads a second overnight bag into the back of our car. When he starts telling me how much we need the opportunity, I pull the wool hat down over my ears. Hardly listening when he tells me the pay is good. Tells me that with this one job, we'll have enough money to stay here for another few months, as if that's what I want to hear.

"You're leaving me here," I say in disbelief.

He finishes arranging his travel bags in the backseat and closes the door. Walks over to me and puts his hands on my shoulders the way he's done my entire life whenever he's let me down. "Hannah, you know I wouldn't if there was any other way," he says.

I pull away.

The dull pain from where I hit my head, once against the ground then once against the lockers, starts to throb. The cold air starts to sting my skinned palms and my eyes grow heavy with the burden of my own rotten luck. In the movies, it never works this way. Whenever anything terrible happens, the characters are rewarded with something even better afterward. Like if they get robbed then they win the lottery the next day. Or if they get in a bad car accident on the way to the airport, it always turns out that it really saved their lives because the plane they were trying to catch crashed and everyone on board was killed. That kind of stuff never happens to me, though. If something really shitty happens, something just as bad is waiting for me around the next corner. That's how this day is, my dad waiting for me with the news of his departure as soon as I make it home from the cheerleading tryouts.

"You promised," I say quietly.

He promised no more trips out of town.

He promised no more leaving me alone.

No more courier jobs no matter what.

He swore to me that he'd never do it again after the last time. He knows I hate being left alone. Coming home to an empty house every night gives me the creeps. Sends me into panic attacks at the slightest noise in the middle of the night and I can never sleep until I run around bolting all the windows. It's bad enough when he's done it in places where I had a lot of friends, but here I'm truly going to be alone among the ghosts that lie tucked into the hollow houses of Maplecrest.

"Don't be like this." He's saying it in a soft voice that drifts down the empty street. "It's hard enough, without . . ."

"Without what?" I snap. "Without having to think about my feelings?"

I snatch my backpack up off the ground. Start to stomp up the driveway toward our dilapidated brown house with its promise of strange noises and shadows that move beneath the wallpaper to keep me company for two weeks.

"C'mon, Hannah," he pleads. His eyes try their best to remind me that we're a team. The same old silent speech about sacrifices I've heard since I was ten years old. "We need this," he says, the car keys dangling from his fingers like a starting gun wanting to get on the road.

"Yeah, maybe I need you," I say, not able to keep my voice from cracking as the syllables slip out through sobs.

His shoulders sag and his mouth makes an O shape without actually saying it. He's finally remembering about me. Remembering that he hasn't even asked yet about my day. After he'd encouraged me all through breakfast, convincing me that it was the best thing to do. That I might make some friends if I participated in the activities that the other kids did. Making me feel like I had a chance and now he's not even going to stick around long enough to help pick me up.

"Didn't go so well, huh?" he asks. Says he's sorry for not thinking about it earlier.

But I won't let him apologize.

Not now.

It's too late for that and I turn my back and start to walk toward the door. He starts saying something. Wants me to come back, but I ignore his request for me to wait. "Forget it, just go," I say.

But he'd never leave things that way and I know it. He catches up to me. Grabs me with both hands and wraps his arms around me. Hugging me even though I refuse to hug him back. Refuse to even look at him.

"Hey . . . I'm sorry," and the worst part about it is that I know he's telling the truth. And I know he's right about us needing the job and the money. Doesn't mean I'm not mad at him, though. Mad that he gets to run away from his troubles but I always have to stay and face mine.

"It's okay, I'll be fine," I tell him, speaking into his coat.

He hugs me tighter before finally letting me go. Telling me he's left some money on the counter for food. Promises to call whenever he has the chance. I nod and watch as he climbs into the car. I sit down on the front steps as the engine roars to life. He waves as he backs up. I put my head down as the car drives off in a cloud of exhaust fumes, wishing I didn't have to spend almost two weeks alone in this place.

I sit there long enough for the sky to change. The pink glow of sunset taken over by the purple clouds of evening twilight. Long enough for the shadows of the trees to stretch from our side of the street to the other side where they fall on abandoned lawns of dead houses.

I can feel the cold in the soft center of my bones like a lullaby. I bring my knees up to my chest and lie down with my backpack tucked under my head. The books beneath the thin fabric like a pillow made of brick. Uncomfortable but still it feels nice as my body starts to freeze. The aches and pains from this afternoon slowly fade. I'm almost able to forget about the series of embarrassing events and leave them for dreams when the footsteps of someone approaching from the sidewalk and trampling through the fallen leaves on our lawn interrupt and spoil my frostbitten sleep.

"Hey," he says like it's a question because he's not sure I'm going to say anything back or just get up without a word, leaving him standing there with his hands in his pockets.

It seems like too much effort to stay angry and so I give in.

"Hi, Lukas," I say, the way I've seen mothers forgiving their kids after they've done something wrong. I don't bother to sit up, but I pull my feet closer to me as a way of inviting him to sit down.

He doesn't sit, though. Shoves his hands deeper into his pockets and does his best to look everywhere but at me. "Look, I'm sorry . . . about what happened at lunch and everything," he says.

"That's okay," I say. "I am, too."

The wind picks up in the distance. I can almost see it as it rolls over the hills and enters the valley. Blows against my skin and scatters our apology like it scatters the brown leaves over the ground, and we both put it behind us just like that.

Lukas puts his hands up to his mouth to warm them as he nestles into the little corner of the porch steps that I vacated for him. His skin looks paler in the shadows. Almost ghost white against the heavy black sweatshirt that he always wears like a second skin. A warmer one. One that hides him in a constant shade.

"How'd it go?" not daring to look at me as he asks. He stares at the empty driveway instead. The fresh oil spot making gasoline rainbows in the air where my dad's car was only a few minutes ago and I'm glad Lukas came by. Glad I didn't send him away because he's actually the only one who cares. Cares enough to ask even though he hates the idea that I went through with it.

I roll over on my back and stare up at the underside of

the awning that covers our front door. "About as well as you said it would," I say, sounding disinterested as I study the flaking remains of a wasp nest left over from a summer some time ago. My cheerleading dreams in a similar state of deterioration.

"I'm sorry," he says.

"No, you're not," I say back to him.

I can see the start of a smile as he lets his head drop from his hands and looks down at his tattered shoelaces. Not the kind of little-boy smile he normally has, more like the smile of an old man smiling at the stupidity of someone younger. "You're right, I'm not," he says and can't help himself from laughing.

I sit up and hit him halfheartedly. "You're a jerk," I say but I can't keep from laughing, either. I guess it's about the only way left to look at it. At least with him. Laughing about it is what will make us friends again. And it actually feels good to laugh. Feels good to have someone to laugh about it with. It makes the whole thing seem less serious. Besides, I have a whole ten days alone to feel miserable.

I move closer to him until our bodies are leaning together like we're Siamese. Rest my head on his shoulder and let out a deep breath and he can tell I'm more upset than I let on. Puts his arm around my shoulder as the last rays of sun go down and the first stars poke through the sky like moth holes in an old blanket.

"Your hands are like ice," he says, wrapping his fingers around mine.

I shiver in response and he helps me up.

"Let's go inside," he says as somewhere down the block a

dog barks and a light switches on in one of the few homes beside mine that is lived in. I do the same, switching on the lamp and filling the room with electric daylight.

I head straight for the couch and wrap myself in its sunken cushions. Lukas circles around the room once. Examining the things lying around like visitors admiring artifacts in a cheap museum. "Where's your dad?" he asks. "Is he going to be back soon?"

I pull my legs up onto the couch and sink even lower. Shaking my head at his total lack of intuition. Even for a boy, he's pretty pathetic. "Shut up and come sit down next to me already," I say.

A confused-puppy look shows in his brown eyes, but he comes anyway. Sinks in beside me and we listen to wind rushing against the roof and the creaking of the beams. Silent and alone together and I have the feeling we're going to get used to times like this.

# EIGHT

**My dad bought me a dream catcher for my twelfth birthday to** keep the nightmares away. I was always having them every time we came to a new house. He told me that he had it blessed by some Native American tribe at a casino. It doesn't work at all, though. But it's still the first thing I hang up in my room whenever we move in. It's just a habit, I guess. Besides, I like the way it looks when the sun shines through it. The colors make even the dreariest room look sort of pretty. But the nightmares still find their way through the tightly woven fabric and visit me in my sleep.

Tonight, my nightmare took place in the school gym. I'm not sure if it was any specific gym. More like a combination of all the ones I've ever been in, sort of swirled together the way dreams do with places. But the army of bleach-blond girls in black skirts told me that wherever it was, I was supposed to recognize it as Maplecrest.

They came in a pack and surrounded me as if I were a prop in one of their routines, only in my dream Morgan was the leader ordering the others. She ordered them to tie me to a wooden pillar that sprang up through the center of the basketball court like the trunk of an ancient tree that wasn't there only a moment before.

The rope felt like thick wool. Scratchy and rough as it dug into my skin, deeper each time the girls danced around the beam to latch me tighter to it. I heard the clapping of hands from an unseen audience off in the distance. Clapping to the rhythm of their feet as the cheerleaders skipped like little Candy Land kids around a maypole, like in movies about children in foreign countries that are always filled with songs and fake scenery. My nightmare had a song, too. A singsong chant of "Death" as my arms and legs were bound strong enough to keep me from even squirming.

I notice for the first time that I'm wearing one of the black uniforms.

Streaks of blood trickle down my body where the rope cuts my skin. Cuts my bare stomach and my legs just below the hem of the short skirt. I can see Miranda next to me, smiling the way I remember them all smiling when I was helpless and injured in the grass that afternoon. Smiling like hungry dogs over a crippled rabbit.

Morgan comes closer and I try to turn my head but the rope around my neck makes it hard to breathe if I turn it too far. Her eyes are bulging from her sunken face, the white part swallowing all but a tiny prick of blue, the color of stars exploding. The skin around her mouth is chapped and split and stained pink like her teeth with the taste of blood.

"Now you're one of us," she says, without moving her mouth.

The walls get darker and the gym is not like the gym in my school anymore because the gym is now outside and the fields are filled with fire as Morgan puts her hand on my chest and pushes me. Holds my chest flat so that it's hard to breathe and I struggle for air. Impossible for me to scream and the air is filled with so many sounds like the screeching of heavy machines but it is only the grinding of zombie teeth.

It burns when her teeth penetrate my stomach and tear into my flesh. Teeth working deeper like bloody chainsaws, ripping veins and getting thirstier with each new layer. Painfully peeling back my skin like tearing open Christmas paper. Feels like I'm being licked with the fire tongue of a demon as my body is torn open with bones poking out at all angles when the other girls join in. Their teeth too long and too sharp, made for shredding organs and pulling apart abdomens.

I feel them swallow my hands and swallow my feet and I try my best to scream but I cannot hear anything except the gnashing of teeth and the warm breathing against my face.

The air is like black smoke when I wake up. Black like ink flooding over me as I scream. The impression of electric blue eyes still there every time I blink. Imaginary eyes staring through the window as the dream catcher dangles helplessly against the frosty glass.

I shove my hands under the sheet and feverishly run them over my stomach to make sure I'm still whole. Kick the blanket from the bed and turn on the light in a panic before getting out of bed and rushing to the window. A rustling of branches in the bushes outside trails off into the woods as the nightmare travels on to the next person.

I look at the clock and realize there's no use going back to sleep. I might as well make some coffee and turn the television on. Use the sound of cartoons to wash out the leftover parts of my dream. Wait for the hour to change and then take a shower and get ready for school. Aware that the only good thing about the nightmare is that real life can't ever be as scary.

**One thing I've** learned from my dad is that avoiding confrontation is the best way to hang on to false hope. Like the way moving from town to town to avoid debt collectors allows us to pretend everything's okay once we reach the next home. Problem erased as if it never happened.

I take the same approach through the school day.

I avoid passing Mrs. Donner's classroom all day. I even go out of my way to circle around the outside of the building to get from third period to fourth and happily accept the late warning from my teacher Mr. Boyle. I even smile when he threatens me with detention the next time it happens, because at least I don't have to see Mrs. Donner and hear the sweet-old-lady tone of her voice as she rejects me for the squad.

I make sure to avoid Meredith in homeroom, too. I wait until I'm sure she is already done at her locker before going to mine. Then I wait for the halls to clear out before going into class and sit in the farthest desk from hers so that she can't break the news, either.

I already know I didn't make it.

I'm not kidding myself. The tryout was terrible.

It wasn't just the one fall, but also the way I stumbled through the marching routine, the slight trip I made going into a handstand, and the ever-present attitude of the rest of the girls at even having me there to begin with. But as long as I don't hear it from Mrs. Donner, I can still pretend it didn't go so bad. Keep up the appearance that I still have a chance, which keeps the whispers to a minimum as I walk through the halls. Until it's official, no one wants to say anything too negative about me just in case.

There's one group I can't fool, though. The perfect girls. They know exactly what kind of a fool I made of myself and during lunch they make sure that I know it, too.

Miranda, Maggie's queen henchman of lunchroom character assassinations, cuts in front of me on my way back from buying a diet soda to the table I share with Lukas in the quietest corner of the lunchroom. Waiting until it's too late for me to stop, she shoves her chair back in the aisle. I stumble into her as she stands up. Knock her back into her chair and brace myself to keep from tumbling onto the floor like the can of soda that slips from my hand and rolls under the next table.

"God! Can't you even walk without falling?" Miranda yells. She digs her fingernails into my arm and claws deep enough to leave a mark when I finally get my balance and step away. I can see the deep blue veins running down her arms that are thin like the bones of birds and I wonder how she was able to squeeze so hard that I have to shake the pain from my wrist.

Her identical cheer sisters cover their mouths and whisper to one another between fits of laughter. Behind me, the semipopular non-cheerleader tagalongs start to quip and point, too, as my face starts to turn bright red.

I reach down to pick up the two dimes that I also dropped and Miranda swings around in her chair on purpose to make sure I stagger into her a second time and knock a yogurt out of her hand.

It splatters like dead bugs against a car windshield, burying my twenty cents under its sticky residue.

"What the hell's your problem?" Miranda says, pushing me into the unfortunate freshman nerd who got stuck behind me by sheer circumstance. The lunchroom aide is standing by the cafeteria door, observing the entire incident. Ignoring the whole thing because that seems to be the rule when it comes to jocks. No disciplinary action needed because they are allowed to get away with everything.

Most of the kids nearby are standing now to watch. Hoping for a fight. But those hopes are dashed when Maggie strolls into the cafeteria. Always late so that everyone can see her walk in. Always an entrance like royalty greeting lesser subjects. But the princess smile leaves her lips when she sees me and Miranda facing off like cats ready to claw each other to pieces. She heads right for us with a determined spark lighting up her eyes.

"Miranda, leave her alone," she says in the steady voice of a master commanding her dog to roll over. Turning to me with suspicious eyes that study me like bright blue spies, letting me know I'm being watched. Warning me not to get any ideas that she's taking my side. I only have temporary immunity according to squad rules that say I'm innocent until proven guilty. But after that, I will be fair game once more.

"Fine," Miranda growls. Puts her hands on her hips and sneers in my direction. "But next time you do that, I'll make you lick the floor clean," she hisses to the delight of those gathered to watch.

I sniff up any sign that she's gotten to me and scoot around her. She bumps me slightly, but just strong enough that I step in the sour remains of her lunch. "Poor girl's going to have to buy another pair of five-dollar shoes now," I hear one of them say and I don't bother turning around.

My soda ended up in the hands of one of the football players when it rolled under his chair. I'm ready to abandon it, figure it's lost now that it's in his possession, a jock, an ally of The Blondes.

I walk past him with my head down.

He touches my elbow as I do and I yank my arm away violently.

"Hey," he shouts in response. "This is yours, isn't it?" The can of soda resting in his hand, held out toward me. I narrow my eyes and search him for any sign of a trick. Any clue that he's only waiting for me to get close enough so that he can open it in an explosion of shaken carbonated foam that will rain down on me, but as far as I can tell he seems sincere and I step cautiously closer.

"Thanks," I say as the cold metal passes from his fingers to mine.

And though he's got the same ghost-blond hair and same electric blue eyes, he doesn't look anything like the others. Something kind and gentle that I wouldn't expect after witnessing the on-field violence of the game last weekend. "No problem. And don't worry about them," he says, quietly pointing to Miranda and the rest of the rah-rah idiots. "They treat everyone like that at first."

"Thanks," I say, feeling shy enough to lower my eyes.

He grins to show me he's one of the nice ones. Nods as if to assure me they aren't all obnoxious, that popularity doesn't necessarily equal cruelty in every segment of Maplecrest High.

When I get back to my table, Lukas has his face buried in one of his comic books. So absorbed in it that he isn't even aware of what happened a few tables over and I sigh. "Great to know you have my back," I complain, slamming the can on the table.

"Huh?" he asks, looking up for the first time and confused to find me so annoyed with him.

"Nothing," I say. I'd rather not relive the experience by telling it to him.

"Okay," he says. Then he tells me I should wait before opening my soda since I slammed it down so hard. "It'll fizz all over the place," he warns.

"What would I do without your wisdom?" I ask but he's already reading through the pictures of the book again and it goes in one ear and out the other.

I nibble on the apple I brought and keep an eye on their table. None of them even glance in my direction as they gossip together with sun shining on them, making their hair look like polished halos, and I feel a little sick inside. It's going to be a long year if my dad's job goes as well as he hopes.

Lukas suddenly slides the book in front of me with his finger tracing a gory scene of corpses being devoured by creatures with rotting flesh. I feel suddenly more sick and slide the book back toward him. "I don't want to see that," I say with the taste of vomit deep in my stomach.

"Just read it," he begs and I tell him that I don't want to read it, either. "Look, it says zombies feed off the living and absorb their energy. That's how they get their strength." He flips the page and points to another scene that I refuse to look at. "Over here it says how they try to lure others in. They poison their blood until they become one of the undead. And if they refuse, they eat them, too," he says, shoving the book into my face.

The illustration shows a man pinned to the ground as the ghouls salivate over him. Drops of blood from their open sores drip into his mouth and by the next frame, the man is as disgusting as them. I snatch the book from him, realizing now that my nightmare didn't come from evil spirits. It came from Lukas and his never-ending barrage of gore comics and silly horror stories.

I wrestle the book from his reach and toss it away.

It slides across the floor and strikes against the trash can placed at the end of our table.

"What was that for?" he asks.

"For giving me nightmares, idiot!" I shout with my arms crossed.

He gets up and retrieves the book. He puts it in his backpack after I tell him that if he opens it once more, we'll never speak again. I also warn him not to bring up any ridiculous zombie tales, either. I'm sick of it. If he wants me to believe that crap, I tell him he better show me some proof. "Otherwise, they don't exist. Get it?" I threaten him.

"Whatever," he says. "You'll see."


I'm sorry, Hannah, I'm just not sure there's a space on the squad," Mrs. Donner says with an apologetic smile. She stopped me in the hall on my way to class before I had the chance to change direction. She breaks the news to me as the rest of the school files past on either side in a whirlwind of shuffling sneakers and broken pieces of conversations.

"I was terrible, wasn't I?" I ask.

"No. No, you weren't. You just need to practice," fixing her glasses as she speaks, searching for something positive to say.

I ask her if that means I officially didn't make it.

"Not this year, I'm afraid," she says and lifts her arms, ready to hug me in case I break down in tears as I'm sure many of the other girls who have received the same news in her same words have done before me.

"Maybe next year," I say, putting on a brave smile, and it seems to please Mrs. Donner that I have so much spirit. But I don't mean it. Not the part about trying out and not the brave smile, either. I just don't want her feeling sorry for me. Don't want her to know I'm even upset.

And I know it's stupid to be bummed by it. I've known since yesterday afternoon that this was coming, but that's the negative side of keeping a false sense of hope. You almost begin to believe that a miracle might happen, so it still hurts when the dream is dashed. Not that my ultimate dream was to be a cheerleader or anything. But I didn't really want to go back to being the girl everyone picks on, either. Not sure I have much of a choice anymore.

I drag my feet down the hall as the warning bell rings. The other kids rush past me, racing against late slips and detentions. I look around for a familiar face coming up behind me, but there's no sign of Diana.

Maybe she's already in class. I'm not exactly of interest anymore and maybe our brief friendship was conditional to my being one of the chosen few. Most likely that's the case. I really hope not. I could use a friend but I can't say I'd blame her. What wannabe wants to be friends with someone who has already been rejected?

Our teacher Ms. Earle steps into the hallway to close the door as the late bell rings. She frowns when she sees me slowly walking toward her. "Miss Sanders, I thought we discussed this yesterday," she says, raising her eyebrows and they disappear under the sharp line of her gray bangs clipped in the most boring hairstyle ever invented.

I shrug my shoulders as I walk past her.

Her skin smells like menthol and medicine when she holds up her hand to prevent me from going in. The wind created by all the classroom doors in the hallway closing at once blows the stale scent from her floral-print dress and I politely turn away. "One more time, young lady, and I'll be seeing you after school," she says.

"Fine," I say, without looking at her.

She grunts at my lack of concern but steps aside to let me enter nonetheless. I walk in with my fingers crossed inside my pocket as I look around for Diana. Her desk is empty, though, and I take one more look behind me to see if she's even later than I am, but I only see Ms. Earle as the door clicks into place to start class.

Ms. Earle taps a ruler against her desk to end the conversations going on between neighbors. She waits for silence before calling out attendance. Never looking up from her little book where our names are printed in her neat handwriting. I wait my turn and say "here" with a flick of my wrist when my name is said. She finishes up in alphabetical order without calling Diana's name. Skips over it completely and closes the grade book without another word.

I figure she must know something I don't. Maybe Diana's on vacation. Or maybe she's sick and the office let her teachers know not to expect her. Or maybe Ms. Earle just knows Diana well enough to know she didn't see her. It seems likely given how she paid special attention to Diana yesterday.

I wait until class is over to ask her. Approach her desk quietly as the rest of my classmates hurry on to their next scheduled destination.

Ms. Earle taps her pen against a pile of papers she started grading toward the end of class after giving us a few minutes to start on our homework. "What is it, Hannah?" she asks, sensing me there more than actually seeing me.

"Um . . . I was just wondering if you knew what was wrong with Diana?" I ask.

"Who?" she asks, clearly wanting me to leave her alone with the papers she bleeds with red pen to check off correct answers and marking the wrong ones by crossing them out.

"Diana," I say louder, making sure I don't mumble this

time. But I say it a little too fast and a little too snobbish gauging by the way Ms. Earle squints at me. "She wasn't in class today," I add in a nicer voice because I don't want her telling me she doesn't know simply because she doesn't like my attitude. I even force myself to smile.

Ms. Earle sighs. She opens her attendance book and scrolls through the names with her crowlike finger. Reads through it once and then a second time and I find it strange that she has to do that after the familiar way she yelled at Diana in the hall only yesterday. Then again, teachers do have six or seven classes a day and I'm sure they can't keep all the names straight.

Her finger finally stops on a name scribbled over with black ink.

"Oh, Diana," she says with a knowing smile, "she's not with us anymore."

"What does that mean?" I ask. Memories of death chants and death threats humming in my ears. Visions of razor-sharp teeth tearing at flesh imprinted on the inside of my eyelids and I start biting my nails out of habit.

Ms. Earle doesn't relay anything as sinister as my thoughts, though.

"Transferred? Moved? I can't keep up," she says with a wave of her hand.

The sound of so many FOR SALE signs blowing in the wind echoes through my mind and I begin to understand. Diana's gone like so many others in so many empty houses that stare out onto the streets of this town where moving is contagious. Nearly epidemic and I suppose that's why no one minds. No one gives a second thought to the departed.

"Okay, thanks," I say and Ms. Earle gives me a dismissive grin before going back to grading tests and takes no notice of me as I leave.

Throughout the rest of my classes, I can't stop thinking about it, though. Why wouldn't Diana mention yesterday' that she was taking off? I even got up the courage to ask one of the girls I'd seen her talk to, asking if she knew anything about it. The girl just shrugged. And when I tried to find out more by asking her more questions, she ignored me. Gave me a look as if I was asking about secrets I had no business knowing and walked away.

Maybe I should forget about it.

Maybe that's the way things go here.

Or maybe Diana's dad is like mine and she came home to find a car packed up and ready to hit the road. I know I've left schools without telling anyone before. But somehow, it feels different. Everything in Maplecrest feels different.

# NINE

**The air is cold on my skin as I run into the world after the** last bell rings. There's ice in my lungs as I breathe and I guess winter comes early in this part of the hills. Earlier than I'm used to. Earlier than my thin coat is prepared for as I follow the cracks in the sidewalk toward nowhere.

Not exactly nowhere. I know where I'm going, just don't know where it is.

I've decided to go by Diana's house. Pass by and see if I can figure anything out. Too many strange things have been happening for me not to. Too many coincidences that keep coming back to me. I need to see for myself that it's all in my imagination. Too many zombie stories and too little sleep. If I can just see her, I'll know I'm being stupid. Even if I can only see a moving truck or her shadow through the window. Anything so that I can quiet the part of me that wants to listen to Lukas's theory about brutal massacres and killings and the possibility that I got her in trouble by mentioning her name yesterday. If I don't, I know exactly what nightmare will be waiting in my room when I get home.

Also, it would be nice to know if she still wants to be my friend even if I'm not who she wants me to be. I'd hate it if she doesn't. I'd like to have one friend in this town who isn't completely psycho.

I follow the power lines into the center of town. Shade covers the storefronts as the sun stays hidden behind a gray sky. The lights inside switch on, dancing with one another across Main Street, where the wind blows colder between the buildings built closer together in this one section of town. Closer together but still lonely. Only the sound of my footsteps to break up the tranquility as I walk toward the pharmacy.

The door chimes as I open it. The cold air from outside collides with the heated air forced through the vent above my head and the cashier watches as I walk over to the bulletin board. The phone directory for the town is there on a little table and I pick it up, flip through the white pages, reading the name ranges printed across the top until I get to the right page and find Diana's.

I tear out a corner from a page in my notebook and copy the address, 16 Timbercrest Drive. It's two streets over from mine heading toward the highway. I remember passing it when my dad and I were looking for Walnut Cove on our first drive through town. I close the phone book and put it back where I found it under the constant suspicion of the bug-eyed lady behind the counter. I escape back into the smell of pine trees and burning firewood and try not to look at the cashier's eyes as they follow me down the street from the store's window.

The bare trees stick out against the sky like skeletons when I turn onto Timbercrest Drive. Their branches waving like a forest of dead bones and the clouds gather thicker and darker like being caught in a ghost story. It makes me shiver and I pull my arms closer to my body to keep the cold from getting in. I'm not too far now. The house numbers counting up by twos, even numbers on one side and odd numbers on the other. FOR SALE signs as frequent as the withered flower gardens, just like the street I live on.

I keep my head down as I walk, afraid to look up. Afraid there's no moving truck in the driveway of the eighth house on the even side. Watching my feet to keep from stepping on the cracks. Crossing my fingers inside my pockets, too, because I'm hoping for some kind of luck to swoop in like a fog that will erase the eeriness of this town when it lifts.

I pinch my skin through the fabric of my coat.

Pinch it harder when I reach her house but it doesn't feel like anything because when I finally bring myself to look, there's nothing there. Only a powder blue house roughly the same size and shape as the brown one I live in.

No cars.

No trucks.

No shadows moving behind closed windows.

The only difference between her house and the other abandoned homes is that her lawn has been kept neat. The leaves have been raked into several little piles waiting to be scooped up and tossed into the woods. The weeds have been pulled from the cracks in the walkway. The hedges have all been trimmed. Even the gardens have a fresh layer of mulch for the winter and I wonder why they would bother with all that if they were just going to move.

That's when I notice there's another difference, too.

No FOR SALE sign hammered into the grass.

I try to tell myself as many rational explanations as I can think up. Like maybe they're on vacation. Maybe a family member died and they had to drive halfway across the country to take care of funeral arrangements. A rich family member, and that would mean they wouldn't need to come back. Or it could be that Ms. Earle was mistaken. I know I haven't known her long, but it definitely seems like she could have a wire or two short-circuiting in her brain. Her eyelids are always twitching and everything, and maybe she's just getting senile.

But, somehow, I know that's not the case. I can feel it. I just know it's something else. Not sure how but I know. The same way I can feel when it's going to snow or when a storm is coming. I have that feeling as I stare at Diana's house and a nagging ache deep in the bottom of my stomach tells me to take a closer look.

My heart races as I make my way up the driveway. The wind picks up, rustles through the branches like the sound of cars speeding by on the highway, as pine needles rain down like matchsticks. A chill runs through me at the thought of peeking in the window and finding rotting corpses with the flesh chewed down to the bone.

I take a deep breath and count to three.

"Stop scaring yourself, Hannah," I whisper as I step onto the front porch.

The stale scent of vanilla perfume lingers in the air like the kind Diana and every other girl in our school wears. Cheap pharmacy perfume that sticks around for days and I try not to pay attention to it as I knock on the door and listen to the silence that follows. I knock harder the next time, more determined and deliberate as if I can summon them to appear simply by applying more force when I strike my hand against the door.

Still no answer and I step off the porch and decide to look in the windows.

A patch of shrubs blocks the windows in the front of the house. I walk around to the side and find a bedroom window. The first floor is raised slightly because the basement is the kind that's only half sunken and I have to stretch to see anything. Standing on my toes, I reach up and grab hold of the ledge. My breath fogs up the glass immediately and I wipe it away. It doesn't make much of a difference. The window is too high. From my angle the only thing I see is the ceiling, so I let go. Trudge through the yard around to the back of the house where there's a sliding glass door that leads from the kitchen. I figure from there I'll be able to see everything.

Even before I get up close to it, I can see the house isn't empty. I see a kitchen table with chairs arranged around it and place mats set out for a meal. I move closer and can see a glass resting on it, too, half full with water and a crumpled napkin beside it. The counter behind it still littered with appliances and dishes. And in the shadows I can make out the outline of a sofa in the living room off to the side and I know for certain that if they're moving, they haven't moved yet.

I hold my hands up to the side of my face and press my forehead against the door. The glare disappears and the inside of the house comes into focus like a television set. Everything is laid out perfectly. Everything where it's supposed to be until I look more closely.

A broken glass on the floor by the kitchen sink.

A chair turned over in the living room.

My hands start to tremble as I discover the signs of a struggle. I've seen enough crime shows to know that something happened. Something terrible. The nagging feeling inside me turns to panic at the thought of so many horrible possibilities. Maybe it's just like Lukas said. Maybe no one really moves away. Maybe the Death Squad goes from house to house murdering those who they don't want around anymore.

I try to take a deep breath but each one comes out quick and frightened. What if they're still inside? What if someone sees me? I try to run but my legs are shaking and paralyzed.

Something flickers in the reflection off the glass. My eyes follow it like a shooting star and I see a shadow looming behind me. A person. A man. And I try to scream but his arm grabs me from behind. An arm around my waist like a rope tying me to a stake and I try to make a noise but it doesn't sound like anything. Meek and mild like a mouse's.

A nauseous sweat breaks out around my mouth as his other palm holds my jaw tight.

His arms are strong like concrete and I feel lifeless as he drags me away from the door. Spins me around to face him and I find myself staring at a pair of eyes hidden by sunglasses the color of midnight. Eyes like the black holes of skeletons and smiling teeth the color of bleached bones. A badge pinned to his chest in the shape of a star that sparkles like a halo even on a cloudy day.

It's okay. Calm down," the sheriff says over and over as I continue to scream into the palm of his hand. The salty taste of his skin on my tongue fades as I close my mouth. Breathing through my nose in short, fast bursts like a trapped animal, but slowly starting to return to normal as I realize who he is. The badge clipped to his shirt telling me everything I need to know.

Once he's sure I'm relaxed, he takes his hand away from my face and releases his grip around my waist. I take a step away from him, my hands shaking as my heart pounds inside me, every tiny hair on my body standing on end.

If there's one thing I don't trust, it's cops. Not after what they've done to my dad. It wasn't fair how they shut him out for trying to do the right thing. Turned on him when he turned in some dirty cops he worked with. They're as bad as the cliquey girls in school. Spreading rumors about him that follow us wherever we go, even into the smallest towns a million miles away from the city we used to live in. They're always giving us a hard time and preventing my dad from doing the job he likes. Sometimes pestering us so much that it's the reason we move. Giving my dad tickets for things he didn't do. Questioning him about crimes that never happened. Free to harass us because there's no one to police them and so I never trust them.

Not ever.

I especially distrust one who would sneak up on a girl and scare her half to death like the one standing in front of me with a creepy smile and invisible eyes.

He cocks his head to the side and folds his arms. His legs planted firmly in my path to keep me from running away as he stares at me. I look small and weak in his mirrored sunglasses. And I know that on the other side of those dark lenses I look like a potential criminal. A teenage misfit snooping where she doesn't belong.

"Now, why don't you tell me what you're doing here," he says. His voice is like a car grinding gears. A deep metallic sound like electronic thunder played through worn-out stereo speakers.

"I . . . I was just . . . ," stuttering and growing smaller in his eyes as I put my hands up to my mouth to try and keep them from trembling. I swallow my nervousness as best I can and continue. "I was checking up on my friend," managing to get it out without tripping over the syllables.

The sheriff scratches the stubble on his face, considering my story as his other hand comes to rest on his hip, inches away from his gun. "You knew the girl who lived here?" Questioning me like a suspect.

"Sort of," I confess.

I can sense that he doesn't entirely believe me.

I keep blinking and looking around because I don't like the way he looks at me. It makes me uncomfortable that I can't see his eyes but that his head moves slightly from side to side. It feels like a million tiny spiders are crawling under my skin as he checks me out the way boys do. Only he's not a boy, he's a strange man with no one else around and a tin star that gives him the right to do whatever he wants. It freaks me out a little and I try to look anywhere but at him. I'm aware it only makes me seem guilty of something, so I try to stop myself. Stare him down and wait in nervous silence for him to say something.

The sheriff's chest heaves slightly when he clears his throat. He cocks his head again, first to the left and then to the right and I can hear the bones crack in his spine. "You're that new girl? The family that just moved in?" His lips barely move as the words escape through clenched teeth and a sneering smile.

I nod, telling him what he already knows.

I've always tried to tell my dad that it's impossible to hide in a small town but he never listens. Doesn't take long before the police know who we are, checking up on us to make sure we're not grifters come to swindle them out of money, like in so many books that I've read. They look into our past and know everything about us before the last of our stuff is put away.

The sheriff approaches me and I flinch.

He laughs and throws his hands up to assure me he has no intention of doing me harm. It puts me only slightly at ease. "Sorry to scare you before," he says and I think it's about time he apologized. "I was driving by when I saw you duck around back," he explains. "Never can be too sure about burglars after people move out."

"They moved out?" I say, rolling my eyes and pointing to the furniture that sits in the house, waiting for people to come home and find it useful. "But . . . their stuff is here."

"Yeah, that's why I was checking up," he says. "They asked me to swing by. Lot of people around here wait until they've settled somewhere, then send for their things later."

He hooks his thumbs into his belt as he staggers past me, brushing me with his elbow as he does. I watch him test the sliding door by giving it a tug. It's locked and he seems satisfied. Never bothering to notice the chair tossed aside or the glass shattered on the floor. I point them out to him as nicely as I can without making it seem like I'm telling him how to do his job.

His face puckers up and he shakes his head.

"Nope, it's probably nothing. Probably just in a rush to leave."

I've spent most of my life in a rush to leave and never left a place looking like that. I keep my mouth shut about it, though. Let the wind blow my hair into my face and I feel safer watching him through the strands like a tiger hiding in the tall grass of the jungle.

"It's sad really," he says, but nothing about his voice sounds sad to me as he goes on about how small towns are dying. "Part of my job is protecting empty houses because no one cares about their community anymore," he says with a grunt of disgust, tapping his knuckles against the side of the house in hatred of all those that disagree with him.

He leads me away from the door. His arms spread like a bird shooing back a predator and then follows me around to the front of the house. The police car is parked in the street, black and white like a zebra without the stripes, and he walks over to the trunk and opens it. From the sidewalk I can just make out the outline of a bundle of FOR SALE signs stacked like luggage as he takes one out and places it carefully in the lawn.

I bite my lip as he hammers it into the ground, the frozen dirt yielding to the metal spikes at the bottom of the sign. Seems like a strange job for the sheriff to be doing. Strange like everything else in this town and he catches me looking at him. He can tell what I'm thinking by the way my eyebrows are raised and he stands up straighter. Tall and threatening, with the trees like blades slicing at the horizon behind him.

"Where is it you live again?" he asks. "I'll take you home."

"That's okay." The thought of him knowing where I live makes my skin crawl. Besides, the last thing I want is for him to find out my dad is away. He looks like the kind of cop who wouldn't think twice about taking me away to some orphanage. "It's not far, I can walk."

"It's no problem," he says, taking another step closer. "I'd really like to meet your father, anyway. He was a cop, right?" I tell him that was a long time ago, but I say it too fast and too defensive. He removes his sunglasses and stares at me through eyes the color of water. Sunken eyes surrounded by a soft pink glow and all the air rushes out of my body.

I slowly start to back away.

"He's not home . . . not right now," I say and concentrate to keep my feet moving. "I'll tell him you want to meet him sometime." Then I say good-bye and wave, turn around and force myself to keep from running. Glancing over my shoulder once I'm a few houses away. He's still watching me and I start to walk a little faster without making it look obvious and by the time I turn the corner I hear the engine come to life.

The car drives off in the opposite direction.

I start to breathe easier when the wind takes the noise away and carries it off over the hills. Hurrying all the way back to my house, I lock the door behind me and sink to the floor. Watch the shadows creep across the room and try to lose myself in their safety.

**By the time** the water for my dinner is boiling, I'm already mad at myself for getting so carried away earlier. I dump the dried noodles in the pot, watch the bubbles drown, and shake my head at how silly it was to get so scared. This is exactly why I made my dad promise not to leave me alone anymore. Every time he does, I let my imagination dream up the most outrageous plots.

I should know better by now.

I should know nothing as interesting as murder would happen in a little town like Maplecrest. That doesn't mean it's not weird, though.

The way the sheriff snuck up on me and all those FOR SALE signs stored in his trunk like dead bodies certainly wasn't normal. His eyes weren't normal, either. The same hypnotic eyes as the cheerleaders and the football players and the creatures in Lukas's comic books.

I pick the pot up off the burner in a fit and slam it down.

"STOP IT!" I shout.

I have to put it out of my mind or I'll drive myself crazy. Concentrate on making dinner. I drain the water from the pot, leaving only the noodles. Stir in the salt-flavored packet and watch the colors change from white to brown as the noodles soak up the taste. Then I turn on the television and hope it will distract me.

I spend the next few hours happily flipping through boring shows about the junk people find in their attics, cars that have better televisions than the one I'm watching, and sixteenth-birthday parties that cost more than the house I'm sitting in. It's comforting in a weird way. Reminds me that these people are more like zombies than the people in Maplecrest. Brainwashed and dumb and I finally feel dulled enough to get some sleep.

I go around and turn off the lights in every room. Double-check the lock on the door in the front and back of the house and even the windows just to be safe. As I'm debating whether to bother washing up the dishes or not, the phone rings.

It's my dad.

I know before answering it because it's too late for salesmen or surveys or bill collectors and no one else would call here.

"Hey, Dad," I say when I bring the phone to my ear.

"Hey," he says and it's nice to hear the sound of his voice as he asks how I'm holding up. I can hear the traffic in the background and know he pulled over at a rest stop to call me. I picture him leaning against a pay phone, one hand on the phone and the other pressed to his ear to block out the noisy background. He seems so lonely when I imagine him that way. I give up on the idea of trying to hold any kind of grudge against him and simply tell him I'm fine. I can hear him smile. I know that doesn't make much sense, but it's the truth.

I almost tell him about the sheriff but decide to keep it to myself until he comes back. He'd just get all panicky and I don't want him to worry. Not if I don't have to.

"School any better?"

"One more day is over, that's something," I say and he seems happy to hear I'm back to my old pessimistic self.

We talk for a little while about nothing in particular. He tells me about the traffic around New York and how he's so glad we don't live anywhere near there anymore. I tell him about the bug-eyed woman in the pharmacy and how I nearly expected antennas to sprout from her head and he laughs. "You find the strangest-looking people in small towns," he jokes, but something about it makes me pause.

It's always been true about the places we've been. The little towns lost in the hills are filled with lumbering, crooked-toothed hicks. So many of them that I lose count.

And that's when I realize what's been bothering me about Maplecrest. It's the fact that it's not filled with those kind of people. There are more beautiful people here than anywhere else. So many pretty girls that it doesn't seem natural.

"I'll try to give you a call tomorrow," my dad says. "If not, then definitely the day after."

"Uh-huh," I mumble but my mind is still trying to wrap itself around the puzzle of an attractive population in the middle of nowhere. It's like anyone who isn't perfect is pushed out one by one until the pretty ones have themselves left with a small town of perfection. Secluded by the mountains and with nothing to attract visitors so that they can create their own little utopia where time stands still.

It makes me sick to my stomach.

A recording breaks up our phone conversation. The voice demands more money if we wish to keep talking but we have nothing left to say, anyway.

"Good night, Hannah," my dad says.

"Drive safe," I say and hang up the phone.

I stand still in the kitchen for a minute, staring at the dishes in the sink. My fingers still lightly pressing against the receiver as all the events of the past week start playing out in my mind and connecting themselves, getting tangled together like the threads of a spiderweb. The way Diana told me I was destined to be one of them was like she was telling me something that I wasn't supposed to know. Then she disappears, just like that.

It's almost like the book Lukas made me read at lunch.

It's almost like someone took her away for leading me closer to the truth.

I feel like it's all starting to come together when my concentration is broken by the sound of branches scratching against the window. It startles me out of my thoughts as I snap my head around in the direction of the noise. The sound of leaves being crushed under footsteps just outside the walls. The sound of being watched by hidden eyes. A sound that takes away the calm I'd worked so hard at obtaining throughout hours of mindless television.

I turn off the lights and stay close to the wall. My back presses flat against it and I hold my breath, hoping whatever it is will go away as long as it doesn't see me.

In the darkness I can only hear quiet and I begin to hate myself all over again. "It's probably just a raccoon or a squirrel," I whisper out loud, hoping it will make it feel more convincing. Then I repeat it. I tell it to myself enough times until I feel brave enough to walk over to the window and press my face to the cold glass.

Nothing stares back at me except the moon and the stars.

Nothing out there but the creatures in my imagination.

I decide to go to bed before I have time to dream up anything else to frighten me. But as I step into my room, I catch the tail end of headlights traveling across the ceiling in a purple and blue pattern filtered through the dream catcher hanging in the window. Only the red brake lights turning off my street are still visible by the time I look out.

"I'm not crazy. Someone was here," finding the sound of my own voice soothing. Someone was watching. But I'm not stupid enough to kid myself into thinking it was anything different than when we lived in Pittsfield or Burbank. They left when they saw me because they weren't looking for me.

They never are.

I should've known all along. There's no ghost story in all of this. This is all about my dad. It's always the same story once we're found out. People we owe money to always coming by at strange hours demanding this or that.

They'll keep coming back until they find him at home. They're never dangerous. Not usually, anyway. Still it pisses me off. As if I didn't have enough problems, now I have to deal with this. I wrap my arms around my pillow and let myself fall on the bed.

Next time my dad calls, I'm going to stay mad at him no matter how lonely he sounds!

# TEN

Lukas comes by my house in the morning before school. I'm in the middle of wasting time with the usual routine of making little trips back and forth from the bathroom to the television while getting ready when he rings the doorbell. He asks if I want to stop at the diner and get breakfast. The options in my pantry aren't exactly appetizing, but the amount of money I have isn't exactly the kind that will last long if I make trips to the diner, either.

"I don't know," I say in a way that lets him know he could still convince me. Ready to wiggle out of my slippers and into my shoes if he says the right thing to help me change my mind.

"My treat," he says and those are the magic words.

"Give me one second," I shout, leaving him at the door.

I grab my stuff, kill the TV, slip on my shoes, throw on a coat, and meet him outside. On the way there, I decide not to tell him anything about yesterday. Especially about Diana. I know what he'll say and I'm not in the mood for all that gore this early in the morning. I just want some pancakes and coffee and to talk about normal things.

I made my mind up last night when I was lying in bed with my eyes open, no more talk about conspiracies or ghouls. I have real problems to deal with, I don't need to add made-up ones to go along with them. I have a dad who drives halfway across the country, leaving me to deal with the creeps we owe money to. I'm attending a school where the most I can hope to achieve is total outsider status. I have a friend who may or may not have vanished under mysterious circumstances and a sheriff who thinks I'm a troublemaker. The way I figure it, that's enough.

The brick buildings on Main Street catch the dawn's light coming over the mountains. They borrow the color of the sunrise but still somehow manage to look run-down. The painted store signs are chipped and flaking. The foundations are all cracked and sinking. Even the diner's metallic silver finish looks less like a star in the sunlight and more like a relic rusting with age.

"This town really sucks," I say as if finally realizing what I've sensed all along.

"Yep," is all Lukas says as he holds the door open for me.

I lead the way to the nearest empty booth, slide into the seat, and he slips into the one opposite me until we're both up against the window. The waitress comes by right away asking what we want. She scribbles down our order and disappears in the clatter of dishes and the low rumble of conversations happening all around.

Lukas and I spend time talking about our geometry teacher and take turns impersonating the frog face he makes when he talks. Lukas is good at it. He's able to make his ears wiggle the same way our teacher does and I start laughing. But my mood quickly changes as Lukas's face returns to normal and he turns his attention to the diner's entrance.

"Don't look now, but your best friends are here."

I hold up my spoon and see the reflection of four blond figures stretched like taffy, the way people look in a fun-house mirror. They slowly shrink to normal size and proportions as they head toward our table. Heading for me and I hide my face with my hand, hoping they'll pass by without noticing.

No such luck.

The sound of their shoes stops inches away.

I turn my head and see Maggie Turner standing there as the other girls with her giggle and keep walking, taking a table on the far side of the diner. Maggie has her hands in the pockets of a long sweater coat that matches perfectly with the knitted hat outlining her face with soft fur the color of snow like her skin. Smooth as porcelain and strawberry lips like a favorite doll. "Hi, Hannah," she says with the kind of smile that makes boys fall in love with her at first sight.

I feel myself sink into the booth, feeling suddenly smaller with her standing over me. Feeling more self-conscious and inadequate. Feeling like this is some kind of trap, too, so I don't say anything. I simply grin, making sure I keep my mouth closed and slightly unfriendly.

Maggie makes the same face back at me. Only on her it means something altogether different. It has nothing to do with being shy like with me. When Maggie makes that face, it's like a mother who feels bad about the way her kids have treated me. It's like an apology without having to say it.

"I don't want to interrupt you," she says, glancing at Lukas, who refuses to wipe away the hatred glaring from his eyes, fierce and ready to protect my honor in the face of female treachery.

"What do you want?" he snaps at her.

The pink skin around Maggie's eyes grows irritated and mean. She stares him off before turning back to me. The glow of her skin switching back to something soft and kind. "I just wanted to let you know that Mrs. Donner was wrong yesterday. The rest of us talked . . . and well, we want you on the squad."

My mouth drops open. I can feel the blood pulsing through the veins in my temples and it's like the world stops spinning for a moment as everything falls into slow motion. So slow that I have a hard time understanding the words she's saying. Then things begin to speed up again and I'm sure I heard her correctly, but I don't believe it.

"Are you kidding or something?" I say.

Maggie laughs and shakes her head. "No, you were really good," she says with the face of an angel that could never lie. "Sure you messed up a few times, but we could tell you have ability. And besides that, we think you're obviously too cute not to be one of us," she says, winking at me.

I refuse to let myself believe her, though, until she rests her hand on mine. An electric warmth rushes through her skin to mine and all the plans that I'd given up on begin to light up again like so many sparks in a fireplace.

"You're serious?" I say, smiling for the first time.

Maggie smiles back, this time like a sister or a best friend, and it's all the answer I need. I can feel Lukas staring at me and I ignore him. I won't let him make me feel guilty for being excited. I won't let him ruin the one good thing that's happened to me in the last few weeks.

"All the girls are dying to congratulate you," she says.

"Even Morgan?" I ask, remembering the way she acted in the locker room. "And Miranda?" I feel queasy as a flashback from the lunchroom plays out in my mind.

Maggie waves her hand in a gesture to let me know they're not important. "Don't worry about them, they'll come around," she says.

"I don't know what to say," I admit.

"How about thanks?" Maggie says.

"Okay, thanks," I say. I can't hide how happy I am and I feel stupid sitting there with a smile that takes up my entire face. It seems to please Maggie, though, and she invites me to sit with them if I want. Making it clear that she means me and only me and so I tell her I can't. "Next time," I say and she makes me promise before leaving us alone.

The silence that follows is pretty much what I expect from Lukas. And him looking out the window instead of at me, that much I counted on, too. It won't change my mind, though. I'm not going to pretend to hate all of them just because he wants me to. I'm sure most of them are fine if he'd give them a chance. Or at least I want to find out for myself. I hate when people prejudge me, so I'd be a hypocrite if I did it to them.

And though I don't dare say any of this to Lukas, I don't

try to hide my excitement, either. I'm actually on the squad! I actually tried something and succeeded. It's a rare accomplishment for me and I'm going to enjoy it.

"Don't let me stop you from joining your real friends," Lukas grumbles at the smile tattooed to my lips.

"That's not fair," I say.

"Yeah . . . well, maybe not," he says as he slides out of the booth. He takes a five-dollar bill and two quarters from his jacket and drops them on the table. The quarters spin like tops before rattling to a stop, tails up. Then he rushes out and I'm left watching him from the window.

I don't try to stop him.

I know he doesn't want to hear anything I have to say. Not right now, anyway. Hopefully by third period he'll have calmed down enough that I can talk to him.


**Maggie introduces the** rest of the cheerleaders to me before homeroom. Motoring off a series of names that all sound alike because they all start with the same letter. I try my best to memorize them all, terrified that I'm going to call someone by the wrong name. I don't want to do anything to mess this up. Don't want to make any enemies on my first chance at being popular.

I feel like a puppy surrounded by children on a playground as the cheerleaders swarm around my locker. Getting attention from all sides and I don't know where to turn or what to say. Maggie's like the proud owner, showing me off and making sure everyone gets a turn to pet me. She stands next to me and makes sure I'm not smothered as each girl pushes closer to make me feel welcome.

Not every girl. A few keep their distance. Morgan and Miranda among them. Their sour faces are dead giveaways that if this was a vote, they were on the losing end. But they are far outnumbered by the rest of the girls who are drowning me with niceness and I realize that I'd blown everything out of proportion over the last week. There wasn't a school-wide conspiracy to sabotage me. It was only a handful of stuck-up snobs, and I let them get to me the way I always do.

Whatever.

It doesn't matter now. Their insults don't mean anything anymore because I'm being showered with compliments from everyone else. And I sort of take pleasure in Morgan's and Miranda's tragic expressions as they linger in the background, having failed to turn the world against me.

I hear Meredith telling everyone how she knew it from the first time she saw me. Some of the other girls are complimenting her. I'm her first recruit. I guess you need to be invited onto the squad, and if someone makes it, it's just as big a deal for the person who recruited her as it is for the recruit. It also means she's sort of responsible for making sure I know the rules. That's okay with me. She's probably who I would've picked if I had the choice, anyway.

I take in the voices swirling around me like the humming of birds. Trying to keep up with who is saying what but getting lost as the words spin around like a carousel, bouncing off the painted lockers, painted doors, and painted cinder blocks that line the halls.

"Where are you sitting at lunch? You're going to sit with us, right?'

"Of course she is."

"Isn't that sweater great on her? It's the perfect color."

"It would look terrible on me."

"Where else would she sit?"

"I have an outfit that would look *amazing* on you."

"Make sure we save her a seat."

"I'll bring it in tomorrow. You can totally borrow it forever."

Everyone is speaking at once and I don't get the chance to answer any of them. I can only stand there as my eyes dart back and forth and grow dizzy.

"Okay! Leave her alone already," Maggie shouts. She tells them there'll be plenty of time to get to know me, but that she and I have to go see Mrs. Donner before homeroom. Then she leads me away as a last flurry of congratulations follow us.

I can instantly tell the difference between walking down the hall with Maggie and walking alone. People step out of the way, staring and whispering as they part like in a movie when royalty passes through the castle courtyard. I've never been popular enough to experience anything like it before. It's a strange feeling, but one I'm certain I could get used to.

Maggie goes over the schedule for the rest of the week. I try to keep track, but quickly get lost. Too many times and places and dates for me to keep straight. Maggie tells me not to worry, that it's all written down. She says Mrs. Donner will give me a paper that has it all printed up neatly.

"Oh, I almost forgot," Maggie says when we get closer to

Mrs. Donner's classroom. "My dad said you were really nice when he met you yesterday."

She says it like I'm supposed to know what she's talking about.

"Who's your dad?" I ask.

"He's the sheriff," she says.

"That's your dad?" My voice cracks in disbelief.

Maggie laughs. She's obviously not used to the idea that anyone wouldn't know that. I guess it's something everyone in a town like this probably knows.

I don't know why, but the news makes me laugh, too, as I replay the encounter in my head. It all makes more sense now. Maggie must have told him about me and that's why he talked to me the way he did. That's why he had the same electric-blue eyes as her. Somehow knowing that he's Maggie's dad makes him less creepy. I must have seemed crazy to him. He's not after me or my dad. "You know, I was afraid of him," I admit, laughing about it now that I realize how dumb it was of me.

Maggie smiles. "Yeah, he does that to people," she says and I feel better already. Then I start wondering if she can clear up the last little mystery.

"So, do you know Diana, then, by any chance?" I ask.

"Mmmm-hmmm." She nods. "She tried out like every year, but she wasn't any good. I was actually glad when I heard she was moving. I won't have to put up with her bugging me to get her a place on the squad anymore."

I watch my feet and shake my head.

I could punch myself for losing sleep over any of this.

"I'm sorry, were you friends with her?" Maggie asks,

suddenly realizing that I must have gone there for a reason. "I didn't mean to talk bad about her."

"No, that's okay. I didn't really know her that well," I admit.

"Good. Then we can forget about her," she says and I agree, happy to put the whole thing out of my mind once and for all. Ready to start all over again at Maplecrest as we enter Mrs. Donner's room.

**I watch him** from across the table at lunch. He sits two tables over and his face goes in and out of view as people pass between us. I guess I was too distracted yesterday when he handed me my soda to notice how cute he is. This time I can tell, though. His hair parted in the middle and hanging just next to his eyes like the sad ears of a rabbit, so yellow and soft that I bet it would feel like a stuffed animal under my fingertips.

He doesn't look tough the way jocks are supposed to. He looks softer. Younger. Almost like a little boy but stronger and with dangerous eyes that don't scare me when he sees me looking at him.

I pretend to look away but secretly keep staring at him.

I feel my hand tremble and my stomach flutter when he stares back. The color rushing to my cheeks and making them blush as I try not to smile but can't stop myself. I fight the feeling to cover my mouth and only push my hair away and tuck it behind my ear instead.

I finally blink my eyes and let a smile slip.

I turn away only after his hand comes up and gives me a shy little wave.

"I think he likes you," Meredith whispers in my ear. Her breath is warm and tickles, kept close to my skin by her hand cupped to hide her words from spies.

"Who is he?" I ask, making my lips move as little as possible as he keeps watching. Meredith tells me his name's Greg. He's a junior. She says he's been on the football team since he was a freshman and that he's the only one who's never dated any of the other girls.

"I guess he's finally found one he likes," Maggie says, holding a carrot stick obscenely to illustrate how she imagines Greg to like me, and we all turn redder before laughing.

"Your other boyfriend's not going to get jealous, is he?" Meredith asks, looking over at the other side of the cafeteria where Lukas is sitting by himself, scribbling furiously in a notebook.

I roll my eyes and sigh.

I didn't think this was going to be so difficult. Being friends with both him and them. I mean, I figured they didn't like him and all. I can deal with that. But I thought he would still be like my secret best friend. The person I turned to when I had something serious to talk about. I thought since he was an outsider, he'd be okay with that.

Pretty insensitive, I know.

But it doesn't mean he has to treat me the way he has today. He won't speak to me. Hasn't since he stormed out of the diner and it's like he wants to drive me away. Like he wants me to side with them just so he can be right.

I tried to talk to him in third period but he ignored me.

I even waited for him before lunch. I didn't want him to walk in and see me at the popular table and think that was the end of everything. I would've sat with him if he asked me to. Even if he didn't ask, I would've if he hadn't been rude when I caught up to him and grabbed his sleeve.

"Leave me alone, Hannah," he shouted. "Or do you have another name already? Michelle? Mara? Why don't you just pass me a note once you find out what they're calling you from now on."

I let go of his sleeve and watched him walk away, waiting until he sat down before I went in and sat with Meredith and Maggie and my other new friends.

I still feel bad no matter how much of a jerk he's been. I just wish I could snap my fingers and make him understand but nothing is ever that easy. I just have to keep trying. Eventually he'll see I'm still me.

"Don't worry about him," Meredith says when she sees me sulking. "He's always been a little strange."

I frown at her so that she knows not to make fun of him around me. But still, she's right. I need to forget about Lukas for right now. This is something he's got to get over, not me.

I go back to staring at Greg.

At the moment, he's much more interesting to me. I let myself daydream about being his girlfriend. About the way he'll show me a different side to Maplecrest and make all my bad impressions go away. Then maybe we'll fall in love forever. Get engaged and then married and have kids with soft bunny hair like his.

"I can talk to him for you," Maggie says.

"No!" I shout and Maggie laughs.

"Don't be nervous," Maggie says calmly. "I'm sure he's going to like you. You're one of us now after all."

One of them.

I try to wrap my head around the idea of what that means. The privileges and responsibilities. Being able to get away with things other kids would get thrown out of school for. Making sure I keep up the right appearance. All the things that go along with being popular. It seems like too much to comprehend all at once and I put it out of my mind. I'll have plenty of time to figure it out as I go along. Besides, I never know how long it's going to last. I could move out of here next week as soon as my dad comes back. No need to worry in that case. Just go with the flow.

"Okay, I guess," I say.

"What? You mean you want me to talk to him?" Maggie asks, checking just to make sure.

"Why not?" I say and she tells me that's more like it. Glad I'm finally getting into the spirit of what it means to be one of them, to be a perfect girl.

**A stale scent** like old sweat and cardboard boxes escapes from the equipment room as Maggie emerges with a uniform for me. It's like the smell of the butcher shop next to our apartment building in the city and I'm filled with the memory of passing it by on summer mornings when the heat brought out the worst of the smells, making me gag a little. I try to peek in the room but only a sliver of fluorescent light shows inside as the door closes heavily behind her. "You'll probably want to wash these but you should try them on first to make sure they fit," she says, handing a uniform skirt and top over to me.

"Yeah, it smells like dead mice in there," I say.

The fabric in my hands smells like dead mice, too.

Maggie laughs and says she knows. "I've made Mrs. Donner complain to that lazy janitor a million times but he never does anything about it."

"That's too bad," I say to be polite. Really, though, I only care about having to wear the leftover souls of dead mice against my skin until I can get home and run it through the wash three times.

I put the uniform down on the bench and stare at it.

"Go on already," Miranda barks. She pushes it closer with an anxious shove as time ticks away toward the time we're due out on the field. I stare at the uniform, one hand pinching my lips and the other running my fingers over the stitched M sewn into the sweater vest.

Black as midnight.

Black badge of honor.

A superhero suit that will grant me special powers the instant I put it on.

The other girls are standing around me. Most of them are already dressed for practice and they are waiting to see me try on the clothes. It makes me uncomfortable to have so many eyes watching as I undress out of the clothes I wore to school. Letting them drop in a pile at my feet and I shiver, standing only in my underwear. Pull the uniform top over my head as quick as I can and the static electricity makes my hair stick up on end. I step into the skirt and pull it up over my bare knees until it rests on my hips, a little too snug and the elastic waistband starts cutting into my skin.

Meredith has her fingers pressed against her mouth, smiling at the sight of me draped in black. "It looks perfect," she whispers. The girls nearby seem to agree as they tilt their heads trying to get a good look. Touching the hem here and there as they do and treating me like a doll decorated in their favorite clothes.

"It's a little small," I say, tugging at the shoulder straps digging into my armpits and pulling at where it clings to my stomach.

"Don't worry, you'll lose that weight soon enough," Morgan says. The syllables slithering off her tongue as her eyes move up and down from my legs to my chest. Pointing out all the places where I'm not as thin as the rest of them.

I cross my arms in front of me to hide from her gaze. I can't help thinking about the way their ribs all show through under their skin when they got changed. I feel fat standing there in a uniform too small to hold me. If I stopped to think about it, I'd know it was ridiculous. My dad's always telling me I don't eat enough and when I go to the doctor, I'm always below average on the chart. But knowing all of that doesn't stop me from hating the way my body looks under the scrutiny of an army of blue eyes sparkling in a dusty locker room.

Morgan snickers under her breath once she sees how her words have affected me. She wraps her bony fingers around my wrist and tries to pull my hand away from my stomach to show off how unlike the rest of them I really am, how my bones in my pelvis are hiding under a layer of skin.

Maggie steps between us and stops her. Grabs Morgan's arms and pulls her away from me. Tosses her off like shooing a bug. Morgan huffs in disgust. She can't believe Maggie would take my side. But she doesn't say it, doesn't cross Maggie. She pouts silently before walking away.

"Ignore her," Maggie says. Then she looks me over the same way the other girls did. "It *is* a little tight," saying it more to herself than to me. Then she tugs at the places where the uniform hugs me close and I can feel my breath freeze up. Something about the way her hand feels against my skin is unlike any way I've ever been touched before and I feel more like a doll than before. "Morgan's right, though. After a week of practice, you probably lose five pounds."

"Oh," is all that I can get out, thinking again about how imperfect I must look to them. Maggie must be able to tell. Girls can always tell when it comes to these things, and so she assures me it has nothing to do with me. Says it's not because I need to lose five pounds, just that it's what happens to every girl because the training is so much work. I repeat my "Oh," but this time it's more confident than before.

"And that all starts right now, so let's go," Maggie says in a cheerful voice, urging me to get my sneakers on and shuffling the others out of the locker room for the start of practice.

Meredith waits behind with me, still beaming at the sight of me dressed as one of them, smiling like a proud sister and her pale skin glows a little pinker than usual, hiding the green trace of veins that are visible under the surface. "You're going to be so great out there," she says.

"Thanks," I say, feeling grateful for the encouragement. "I'm still not so sure about this whole thing," I admit as I lace up my shoes. "I mean . . . it's just that I'm not like the rest of you . . . you know what I mean?"

Meredith lets her eyes go soft and sits down beside me. She rests her hand on my elbow. "Yeah, I know," she nods. "We've all known one another forever, it must be kind of hard to jump right in." And I never thought of it like that, but I suppose that might be what it is. Maybe all my nerves and doubts are just because I'm the outsider trying to fit in. "It's like being adopted into a family, it takes time," Meredith says.

"I guess it is," I say, thinking if the rest of the family is as kind as she is, then I'm really going to like being a part of it.

Meredith gets up, offers me a helping hand, and leads me toward the exit. "You'll see," she says as the door creaks open and floods my eyes with the harsh white light of the sun. "You'll blend in before you know it."

A few steps in front of me, Meredith disappears in the glare of the sun. And I think that is how it must be. That we are like the drenched afternoon sky that fades all the colors so that after a while you can't tell yellow from white or blue from green. The squad, standing in four straight lines, blends the same way in front of me so that I can't tell Meredith from Miranda or Maggie from Morgan. The idea of being lost like this used to frighten me, but now I understand a little better and I think it might feel safe and secure to fade into the scenery. It might be nice to have a family for once.

# ELEVEN

The first time I can remember seeing the ocean, I was five years old. I'd seen it before but I couldn't remember. My dad always tells me how he and my mother used to take me to Coney Island when I was a toddler. He said I used to spread my arms like the seagulls and run in the sand, pretending to fly. I don't remember any of that, but I do remember the time we all went to the beach in Virginia the summer before I started kindergarten.

I don't know if it was because we were in a strange place or if I was just finally old enough to have memories that last, but I'll never forget staring at the ocean. It didn't look anything like the way it does in Brooklyn. It looked endless and it looked hungry. The waves were like so many tongues wanting to swallow the world and drag it under.

Cheerleading practice is the same as the ocean, each girl like a wave rolling over one another, struggling to be the first ashore and pulling the others in her wake. The expression in their eyes just as fierce and as hungry and as blue as the water that grabbed for my toes that I kept dug into the sand. And they never get tired, the same way the waves never stopped coming toward me with long, watery tongues wanting to lick my skin. Surrounded by them, I feel just as helpless as I did facing the ocean, waiting to get stolen away.

I had trouble keeping up after the first ten minutes. I couldn't believe how much energy the other girls had. I couldn't figure out where they hid it in their skinny bodies. Strength as measureless as the number of waves in the sea, while I was bent over trying to catch my wind. No one but me ever even seemed to be out of breath, and I could see Morgan making sure everyone else noticed each time I raised my hand and took a break.

On the way back into the locker room afterward, I overhear some of the other girls asking Maggie whether or not I really belong. They're not so sure I'm cut out for it. Not so sure they've made the right choice to let me into their group.

"Did you see her? She'll never survive," a girl named Mandy says.

"We should just get rid of her now," Morgan says.

"Shhhh, she'll hear us," Mandy says but Morgan says she doesn't care if I do.

"I care," Maggie said with an authority that shuts the others up. "I don't want anyone talking about a member of our squad that way."

"She's not a full member yet," Morgan snaps, saying it like a challenge.

"She will be," Maggie growls and I can't help myself from looking over my shoulder to witness the way Maggie controls her with one angry look. And even though it feels good to have her on my side, my mood still sours because I know it's true. I know I still have to prove myself and I wonder how long it's going to take. I wonder if I even have it in me to go all the way through with it or if I'll end up quitting the way I've quit everything in my life as soon as it gets too hard.

Morgan's smirking face passes by me in the locker room. "How's your head?" she says, rubbing her hand at the spot on the back of her own head mimicking where I hit the floor the other day and banged my head against the lockers.

"Fine," I say through gritted teeth and she laughs the way witches cackle at the moon in scary movies as she walks off.

It'll be worth all the sore muscles and sprains just to piss her off. It doesn't matter how difficult it gets, I'm not quitting because, for no other reason, at least it'll make her miserable to have me around.

I finish getting dressed. I don't shove my uniform in my bag, though, I keep it tucked under my arm instead. I don't want it polluting the rest of my things. The dead-mouse smell has only grown stronger in the last hour. Add in the scent of my own sweat and it's toxic. It would last forever if I stuck it in my bag. I'd smell it every time I opened it up to get anything, so it's better to deal with it out in the open for the short walk home. It makes sense to me to suffer a little now to prevent from suffering a lot more later on.

I say good-bye to Meredith on my way out. She asks if I want to go to the diner with her and some of the other girls, but I shake my head. I'm too tired and plus I'm too broke. "Maybe tomorrow?" I say and that seems to make her happy.

"Yeah, sure," she says. "See you later."

I hurry out of the locker room and into the darkening halls of the empty school. I want to get out of there before running into anyone else who might try to persuade me to go along with them so I'll have to sit for hours and gossip. I don't have the energy for it. I don't even have the energy to make up excuses, so I avoid everyone by going out the back way and step outside into the safety of twilight.

It's a relief when the cold air rushes against my skin. The sweat drying into salt crumbs as the wind blows on me and I can't wait to get home and let a warm shower wash it all away. I walk as fast as my legs can manage given the way my muscles are burning with each step. I keep the image of the bathtub in my mind the way a wanderer in the desert keeps dreaming of an oasis, the rust-stained tiles lingering in the air like the promise of presents on Christmas morning.

The image shatters and trickles away the second I see Greg leaning against the brick wall outside the boy's locker room. The security light above his head switches on as the shadows cloud over, tricking it into believing it's night already. Its white light makes him look ghostly, bleaching his skin like an overexposed photograph and all I can see are his eyes. Beautiful eyes like a girl's that burn with electricity with a frightening glow that pulls me toward him.

I scratch my fingers through my hair to comb it into some sort of attractive mess. He smiles at me, pushes himself from the wall, and starts to walk in my direction. I swing my backpack off my shoulder and stuff my uniform deep into its black hole. I'd rather suffer later and have this moment be perfect. Besides, the bag can be washed after all.

"Hey," he says, stopping in front of me.

I stop, too, and say "hi" as shy I've ever said anything. I've never been very good with boys. Flirting with them, I mean. Not ones that I actually think are attractive, anyway. I'm able to do it perfectly with the ones I'm not interested in, or the strange kids who always fall in love with me, like Lukas. There's no pressure there because I don't really care much about the outcome. But when it's a boy that I sort of secretly like, I end up standing with my hands behind my back and trying to look everywhere but at him.

Greg's not too good at it, either, though.

I can tell right away. He keeps tapping his foot against the parking lot blacktop. His hands move back and forth from his coat pockets to his jean pockets and he also tries to look anywhere but at me.

"Are you going to the diner with everyone else?" he asks. He stares at the figures on the other side of the lot heading in the direction of town. It gives me the courage to look at him knowing he's not watching me.

"I don't know," I tell him. "I don't really feel up to it."

"Oh," he says, "that's cool." He shrugs his shoulders and everything but he's not able to hide his disappointment. It's obvious he's been waiting there for me to come out. He's probably been planning this since lunch, thinking that he'd walk with me and then we'd sit together, talk, and fall in love and now I've ruined his daydream.

"Then I'll walk you home," he says, saying it like a command and making his eyes as big as can be so that there's no way I can say no. I don't know why, but I sort of like not being able to resist him. There's something exciting about the way he talks to me. And besides, I'm not sure I don't want exactly what he wants.

"Really?" I ask.

"Really."

"Okay, yeah." My stomach feels like it's turning inside out when I think about being alone with him in my driveway. I stifle a nervous laugh by biting my lip and start to walk in the direction of my house, careful to brush my arm against his so that I can feel the brief contact of our sleeves rustling together when the fabric touches.

A few of the football players pass us on their way to the diner. They point and laugh. I hear them whisper about how Greg's finally got himself a girl. And I'm really glad he doesn't take any notice of them. He doesn't stop and try to show off or act tough, just keeps walking at the same pace as me until we leave them behind.

We don't talk for the first few blocks. Not really, anyway. He asks me typical questions about my first practice. I keep my answers to one word. Okay. Fine. Things like that. Then he coughs a fake cough before asking me if I have a boyfriend.

I shake my head.

Watching my feet as I walk because I don't want to look at him and give away the jitters inside me that are leaning toward wanting one.

"What about that kid you're always hanging out with at lunch?" he asks.

"Lukas?" I ask, pretending to be surprised so I can hide

how excited I am that Greg's been noticing me enough in the lunchroom to know who I sit with. "He's not my boyfriend. He's just a friend," I tell him. "At the moment, not a very good one," I add, thinking about how Lukas would react if he saw me walking home with one of the zombies of Maplecrest.

"I'm sorry," Greg says, lowering his head to show he means it.

"It's okay," I tell him. "I'm starting to think it's not such a bad thing." I'm starting to think Lukas isn't all together upstairs. Now that I've gotten to know some of the kids he's always warning me against, I realize how wrong he is. They're as normal as kids anywhere else. Maybe they're right to call him a freak. Maybe he really is just one of those bullied kids who goes on a shooting spree once they finally snap.

I push the thought from my mind.

I don't like thinking that way about him. It's not fair.

"How do you like it here, anyway?" Greg asks, trying to change the mood as he skips a few steps to kick at a leaf pile on the curb.

"Okay, I guess," I lie. Though it's getting closer to the truth with each friendly smile he gives me.

"Why did you move here? You have family here or something?"

That makes me laugh. Not because it's funny, but because it couldn't be further from the reason. "We don't have family anywhere. No aunts, uncles, cousins, or grandparents," I say. "Just me and my dad." And that makes me laugh, too, though not the good kind of laugh because not even my dad is here. So really it's just me. I might as well be an orphan for the next week.

"If you stay here long enough, you'll have more family than you'll want," he jokes. Telling me that living in a small town has its drawbacks that way. "But I guess it's good, too. We all look out for one another. Protect our own, you know?"

"Like a team," I say.

"Yeah, like a team." He smiles, happy to see that I really do understand what he's trying to tell me.

I step closer to him, wanting suddenly to feel protected and part of the same team as him. His skin looks like a soft sculpture in the first shadows of nighttime. Perfectly smooth except for his chapped pink lips that crack when he stops smiling. I reach in front of me and rest my hands against his chest. He has to wrap his arms around me to hold me up and I can feel how strong he is as I lightly press my mouth against his chin.

The moon pokes through the sky as we stand near my house in each other's arms. My mouth softening his dry lips with a kiss that I never want to end, that I want to go on and on like the ocean off the coast of Virginia, somewhere in my memories.


**I'm still daydreaming** about Greg an hour after watching him follow the sidewalk back into town. I wrap my arms around a pillow as I lie on the sofa imagining myself kissing him over and over again. Kissing him with my eyes closed like in a dream. There's something about the way he kisses that's unforgettable. That stays with me as the clock ticks away into the evening. It's like part of me was swallowed up and changed inside him and I feel different now. Like a series of tiny stars are exploding beneath my skin and tickling me with their sparks.

My dad says that's another part of the teenage-girl sickness. He's diagnosed me with it weekly for the last four years of my life. "First symptoms of a full-blown crush," is what he tells me whenever I tell him about something magical that happens between me and a boy I like. It makes me angry the way he never takes it seriously. But then again, I've had friends whose dads take those things way, way too seriously and I guess I'm sort of glad it's the other way around with mine. Still it gets on my nerves that he never believes in true love, and that most of the time he's right about it just being a passing phase.

He'd be wrong about Greg, though. Even if I've only known him for one day, I know my dad would be wrong.

I hold the pillow closer, hugging it until all the fluff is squeezed out and then I relax my arms. I open my eyes and see the clock staring me in the face. I know I have to get up and make some food. I still have homework that can't be ignored. I need to wash that uniform before it grows moldy, and the shower I promised myself is still waiting for me. But I know if I get up my whole body will ache. I know the phantom feeling of Greg's arms will fade and leave me truly alone.

The return of nightly noises outside the house is what finally forces me to stand up. A scratching sound moving clumsily over the dead leaves on the frozen ground. I watch the ceiling for headlights traveling across the room but there's nothing. It doesn't startle me quite the same as it did yesterday. Even if it is people looking for my dad, I'm not as worried anymore because I have people to protect me. I'm part of a team now.

I get up from the sofa in a quick motion that brings back the memory of practice in the form of a shooting pain that dulls every inch of my spine. I do my best to shake it off and walk to the front door brave and steady because I don't care who it is, I'm not running away anymore. I'm not hiding and I'm not going to be frightened. I open the door as wide as I can and face the darkness, standing up to the wind that rushes against me, doing its best to deter my confidence.

A pair of glassy eyes meets me in the doorway.

"It's you." My voice comes out somewhere in between relief and hatred at the sight of Lukas hunched over on the porch. "Hasn't anyone ever told you not to sneak around a girl's house and scare her half to death?" I tell him, exaggerating about how afraid I actually was.

"Sorry," he mumbles as insincerely as possible.

The door swings slightly in my hand and I'm really close to slamming it shut. I can't believe him. I can't believe the nerve he has creeping around after the way he acted all day and then make it sound like my fault. Moping about like I'm the one who needs to apologize!

"What do you want, Lukas?"

His shoulders slump and his back curls to make his long body into the shape of a question mark as he shrugs. "Nothing really," he says. Kicks at a few stray leaves that have blown onto the brick steps. Shoves his hands deeper in his pockets and glances up at the porch light. "Just wanted to see if you were okay."

"I'm fine," saying it in a way that suggests that though I'm fine, there's something wrong with him. "I don't need you to protect me," I tell him. Trying on purpose to be mean because I'm beginning to think that it was him creeping around yesterday, too. I'm starting to think he's the only thing in this town that I need protection from.

"It's already happening," he says under his breath.

"What's that supposed to mean?"

He stands up straight and looks me in the eyes for the first time. Speaks clearly for the first time and says, "It means it won't be long before you're not you anymore."

"You don't even know who I am!" I raise my voice because I'm not about to go through this again. I've had it with him telling me who I should be and who I shouldn't be.

"Don't you get it?" he shouts back. "I've seen this happen before. You'll get so swept away with being popular that you won't see it coming. By the time you realize what's happening, it'll be too late. You'll be one of them."

"Yeah, well, maybe that's not such a bad thing." Telling him he's just jealous because I'm fitting in. "You're just mad because I don't want to be a freak like you."

He rushes at me and grabs my arm before I can shut the door. Staring at me with crazy eyes and spitting his words. "Hannah, you'll be dead! You'll feed on corpses like maggots do! Is that what you want? Is being popular worth that?" Screaming so that his voice hurts my ears.

"If that was true, you'd already be dead," I shout. "They'd have killed you a long time ago for being such a freak!"

"You don't think they're not going to kill me?" he yells, gripping my wrists tighter so that I can't pull away and slam the door. "You don't think they'll kill me as soon as they're not worried about you getting suspicious?"

I yell at him to stop.

To let go of me and leave me alone.

He only clenches me tighter. Shouts louder as if it will sink in as long as his words drown out every other sound in the world. He's still yelling when the car drives by. And I'm still trying to fight him off when it pulls into my driveway. Lukas doesn't notice the hum of the engine, the click of the car door, or the quick rush of footsteps hurrying up the walkway.

An arm latches around Lukas's neck and cuts off the words in one sudden strangling sound. He lets go of me and clutches at the arm sealing the air off from his lungs as he gasps for breath. The sheriff applies more pressure and drags Lukas a few feet away. He finally stops struggling once the sheriff throws him to the ground like tossing away the trash.

I cover my mouth as he towers over Lukas with his arms folded and his boots ready to kick him if he dares to move. I'm not sure whether to rush out and help him or if I should throw my arms around Maggie's dad and thank him for rescuing me. So I just stand there. Confused and useless.

"You all right?" the sheriff asks in a low voice. His face is split down the middle, half hidden in the shadows while the other side is bathed in electric porch light.

"Yes," I say into the palms of my hands. But I can feel my heartbeat racing throughout my body and everything has happened so fast that I'm not sure if I'm all right or not.

But he doesn't seem too interested in my answer, anyway, turning his attention to Lukas. Bending down so that when he speaks, Lukas will feel the heat of his words. "A real tough guy, huh?" he sneers and Lukas coughs up spit on the ground as he tries hard to catch his breath.

"Don't hurt him," I shout and they both glance at me. Both of them as surprised as me when I say "please."

The sheriff steps away as Lukas stumbles to his feet. The terror in his eyes upsets me and even though I have every reason to never want to see him again, I can't help but feel sorry for him as he starts to jog away. Picking up the pace as the sheriff shouts out a warning for him not to come back. The sound of his feet, running faster, echoes off the empty houses as he passes them before ducking into the woods that cut through to his house.

"Something'll have to be done about that boy. He's always been trouble," the sheriff says. I don't know why, but the tone of his voice gives me the chills. Wondering what he means by *something*. Worried that it means something worse than I can imagine so I tell him the whole thing was nothing. He raises one eyebrow at that and says it didn't look like nothing. Gives me a speech about how girls try to cover for boyfriends who hit them.

I assure him that Lukas is not my boyfriend and that he wasn't trying to hurt me.

"If you say so," he says just like I'd expect from a cop. Maggie's dad or not, he's a police officer before he's anything else and I still don't trust him. I trust him even less when he starts asking about my dad again and keeps trying to look over my shoulder into my house.

"He's not here," I say, and I know right away that it sounds suspicious. "He works late," trying to cover but it only comes out sounding more guilty than before.

"Well, in that case," he says, putting his hands on his hips, "feel free to give me a call if that kid comes back and gives you a hard time."

"He won't. But I will," I say. Then I thank him and begin to close the door. He heads back to the car and stops. Hits his forehead like a forgetful old man on television and turns around. Says he nearly forgot, then congratulates me on becoming a cheerleader. Tells me we're the pride of the town along with the team. I smile and thank him again, though really it doesn't make me happy to hear it. There's just something about him that doesn't feel right. And once he's gone, I start to wonder about him. Wondering why he happened to be here on my street and why he's so interested in my dad. Wondering why he's so interested in me, too, and why he'd bring me up with his daughter the other day. Wondering why he'd be at Diana's house with a trunk full of FOR SALE signs and why he seems to hate Lukas so much.

None of it makes much sense.

I don't know why, but I know I don't like him.

And I know that when my dad calls the next time, I'm going to tell him about it. I'm going to tell him to hurry home.

# TWELVE

I'm getting stronger. After only three practices, I don't need to stop except for once or twice to catch my breath. I'm learning the routine, too. Mrs. Donner says I'm picking it up quickly. Tells me she's glad Maggie made her reconsider me for the squad. She called me *ideal* and I'd be lying if I said it didn't mean the world to me to hear it.

It's not that cheerleading has all of the sudden become my whole life or anything. It's just nice to finally be good at something that everybody else thinks is special. It's nice to be accepted. And I've definitely noticed a difference in the way people treat me since I've started hanging out with Meredith or Maggie, or even Greg. Not just from the kids in school, either. Even in town. Everyone is much nicer to me now.

I know it's exactly the kind of special treatment that would bother me if I saw some other girl getting it just because she was part of the popular crowd, but somehow it's different when it's me.

My dad would make a face at me if I said that to him. He'd get that half-frown, wrinkled-forehead look that he makes when he doesn't agree with me. He'd tell me not to be a hypocrite in the disappointed tone of voice that used to make me cry when I was little. But he's not here to say any of those things, so I don't care what he would think.

"Hello? Are you even listening to me?"

I blink myself away from my thoughts and look at Meredith. She hooks her arm around mine so that we're locked at the elbow as we pass under the fluorescent lights of the abandoned hall. White light that shines down on the speckled pattern of the cheap tile to make it glitter like golden bricks. To tell the truth, it sort of feels that way, too. The last few days have felt like a different world. A better one.

"Sorry," I say with a laugh to shake off my daydreaming. "I'm listening now."

Meredith smirks and narrows her eyes at me. She's getting used to me drifting off. "I *asked* you how you like being one of us . . . you know, being cooler than the rest of the dorks," she says.

"I guess I like it," I say. Slowly as if I'm still thinking about it even though I made up my mind three days ago. Then I laugh so that she knows the "I guess" part of my answer was a complete lie.

"No one's giving you a problem, right?"

I shake my head. Tell her even the teachers are being nice to me and Meredith tells me that's part of the deal. That's part of why everyone wants to be like them.

"How long have you been on the squad?" I ask.

"Forever," she says in an exaggerated tone. "I can't even remember what I was like before."

I grin. I sort of wish I could forget a lot of what happened before.

"Come on, let's go," Meredith says. The rest of the girls are already at the diner waiting for us. Greg's staying a little longer today along with the whole football team. He told me it was their day to lift weights. I couldn't imagine having the energy to do that after a practice but I guess that's what makes them the best.

Meredith unhooks her arm from mine. She catches me looking over at the door to the boys' locker room. "Thinking about lover boy?" she jokes.

"Maybe a little," I confess. It sounds better than the truth. Better than telling her I haven't really stopped thinking about him since he kissed me two nights ago. But Meredith can tell that anyway. No matter what words actually come out of my mouth, my smile gives me away.

We both start laughing as we push the doors open and walk into the soft colors of twilight shining off the cars in the parking lot like a string of holiday lights. As the wind rushes up on us, Meredith tells me for the tenth time today how perfect Greg and I are for each other. If I didn't sort of believe it myself, I'd start to think it was some kind of arranged marriage the way our friends keep pushing us together. But if it is, I guess I'm grateful. I've never had a boy who's so perfect be so crazy about me before.

"Is he coming by the diner later with the other guys?" Meredith asks.

I shake my head.

Meredith's eyes light up in surprise because that's the way it's supposed to work. The boys come by once they're through with being gym rats. Those are the rules but Greg and I decided to break them just a little.

"No," I tell her, "I'm going over to his house when he's done."

I bite my lip to keep from showing how nervous and excited I am. Looking over at Meredith out of the corner of my eyes and letting the wind keep my hair in my face so she doesn't see. But I can see her face. A blue spark of electricity in her eyes. A hungry smile that shows her teeth. And maybe it's just the way the evening sun mixes with the neon glow of the diner's sign, but something dangerous flashes across her face. Then it fades as soon as it came. So quick, like something I wasn't supposed to see, and I can feel my stomach drop the way it does when getting on a scary ride. The panic feeling I get whenever I want to change my mind about going through with something. Because all of the sudden I'm not sure going to Greg's house is a fun idea.

But that's crazy.

I know it's crazy.

I brush aside the hair hanging in front of my eyes and turn to face her. Everything's normal. Her smile is as friendly as it always is and I know I just caught her in one of those in-between faces. Same as it always is when I'm nervous.

"Oh, look, they already got the good table," Meredith says when we get inside the door and see the rest of the girls sitting in the back corner at the big circular booth. They wave to us as we head toward them, moving around to make space for us to sit down.

I look over at the clock hanging behind the counter.

One hour and fifteen minutes until I'm supposed to be at Greg's.

I listen to everyone gossip about our teachers, the boys on the team, and the kids who they're going to hate for the next few days. I join in with an occasional laugh or just to say yeah or something else to show them I agree with everything that's said. But really I'm just watching the clock. Glancing over at it every other minute and hoping for a Cinderella kind of night.

**The lights are** on in every window of Greg's house when I walk up the driveway. It doesn't look like a real house. Not one that anyone lives in. More like a house out of an old painting. Large windows with matching curtains tied back neatly. A wraparound porch with two rocking chairs creaking in the wind, gently like they're being rocked by ghost children. Spirals of smoke billowing from the chimney and silhouetted against the bright moon.

Picture perfect.

The complete opposite of every house I've ever lived in.

Dragging my feet up to the porch, my shadow grows suddenly long and thin as I step into the warm glow pouring from the front room onto the cold ground.

Everything seems so peaceful that part of me wants to turn and leave. Even the quiet tapping of my feet feels like an intrusion. I've never known how to behave in front of perfect people. I barely know how to act in front of a boy that I'm crazy about, let alone his parents. I'm afraid they're going to hate me and make him hate me, too. So I just stand there on the porch with the door inches away. Stuck in the middle of the cold wind against my back and the warm light coming from the window above my head.

I hear Greg's voice on the other side of the door, shouting from the top of the stairs so that his words get tangled up with the noises coming from the kitchen. The clatter of dishes and the sound of running water. The scraping of forks and the shuffling of feet over tile floors. Sounds that are the same in my house and I start to relax. Start to lift my hand and knock.

"Got it," Greg shouts as his feet thunder down the steps as fast as my heart is beating. Opens the door in a fast, sweeping motion and the smell of food escapes into the air. Then I see his eyes. Eyes like snow falling at midnight. Full-moon eyes that have a way of making me melt when they meet mine.

"Hi," I say almost in a whisper.

"Hey," he says as normal as ever. "Come on in." And when he steps aside and touches my shoulder, I know I've made a big deal out of nothing.

I blame Meredith and all the other girls for making me so nervous about this. They wouldn't stop talking about us the whole time at the diner. They made it seem like this was some big test of our relationship or something. At least Morgan made it seem that way. And she also made sure to let me know she was certain I'd fail. Teasing me that I'd say the wrong thing. That Greg would be watching everything

I said and did in front of his parents and would dump me for the tiniest mistake.

I knew she was full of crap. She was just trying to make me so nervous that I would embarrass myself. I know that, but still it isn't until I see him smile for the first time that I start to breathe easier.

"Perfect timing," he says. "I just finished eating."

I try to think of something clever to say. Something funny about how I always have perfect timing, but nothing that I think up sounds funny at all so I just sort of nod and smile.

"Who is it?" his mother calls out from the kitchen. "Who's here?" But she's already poking her head in the doorway before Greg can answer. She's pretty. She doesn't look old enough to be his mother. Or maybe she does, but she doesn't look as old as the mothers of other friends I've had. She has her hair pulled back into a tight ponytail but even from just a glimpse of it I can tell that Greg gets his loose blond curls from her. His eyes, too, and it makes me like her right away.

"This is Hannah," Greg says. The way he says my name makes me smile because the way he says it is so familiar, like it's been mentioned many times to her before.

"Hi," I say, forcing myself not to wave like a shy little girl. "Nice to meet you." Greg's mother smiles politely and says the same back to me before disappearing again.

Greg rolls his eyes and apologizes for her. "Sorry. She's boiling some kind of roast or something for tomorrow," waving his hand dismissively through the air to make sure that I know he's not really sure what she's doing and that he doesn't really care.

"That's okay, I didn't come here to see her," I say, grabbing his hand and pressing my fingers between his so that the feeling of his skin rubbing against mine makes my breath weak for a second.

"Let's go upstairs," Greg says, nodding in the direction of the steps and pulling me there slightly.

"Okay, let's," I say.

He leads me there by the hand and I follow. Turning my head to the wall and looking at the photographs and plaques that show Greg's life. The oldest pictures at the bottom and the newest near the top and I watch him grow up at a dizzying pace. The images passing like the pages of a flip book until we reach the top.

The door to Greg's room is right near the stairs. The door is open and he stands to the side, letting me go in first. It's not the first time I've been in a boy's room. Not even the second or third, or even any number I can remember. But still every time is kind of like the first time. There's just something different about boys' rooms. The colors. The way the furniture is arranged. The things lying around. It takes a minute for a girl to figure out how to find her way around it. Sort of like walking into the boys' bathroom by mistake. It always takes a minute to figure out where you are and what those things on the wall are for.

"I see you didn't straighten up for me," I say as my eyes travel from pile to pile of books and papers and clothes stacked in every corner. Greg laughs. He says he wanted me to see the real him. I laugh, too. Tell him my room isn't much better.

"Sit down. I mean, if you want," he says.

I lower my eyes at him and raise my eyebrows because the only place to sit is on his bed. That's okay and everything. But I just want him to know that I know a trick when I see one.

He seems to know, though.

It's not some kind of trick. He knows exactly what he's trying to do and though it should piss me off, it doesn't. I sort of like that he's not playing a game or anything. Not like some of the other boys I've liked who always fumbled around the question, trying to act all innocent when we both knew what he wanted.

Greg sits down on the edge of the bed and places his hand next to him like an invitation for me to join him. His eyes drawing me closer and it surprises me how easy it is for him to convince me. I hold my arms out like a bird and let myself fall backward on the mattress. Then I let my fingers walk toward his until we're holding hands again.

We both start to laugh and for the first time since I came inside, we both begin to feel normal. Like ourselves. Like we feel when we're alone. Like we're the only two people in the world.

"So tell me the truth, am I the only girl who's ever been on your bed?" I ask, half kidding and half wondering. I already sort of know the answer. The girls have told me all about him. Told me how I'm the first girl he's liked in forever. But that doesn't mean anything. Not really. There could be some secret girlfriend somewhere that no one knew about. And when he answers no in a shy way, I know that there is someone and I perk up.

"Who was it?" I ask. I'm not jealous at all. I'm more excited than jealous. Excited to find out something The Blondes didn't know. I guess since I started hanging out with them, I've gotten a little taste for gossip.

"Just some girl," Greg says. "But we weren't right for each other, you know. Besides, she didn't live here long."

"Oh," I say. Another someone who came and went isn't so exciting. Not in this place. And after my curiosity is satisfied, my jealousy starts to act up. "Was she prettier than me?" I ask.

"Not even close," he says. I don't care whether or not it's the truth, it makes me happy just that he said it.

He reaches over and touches the soft hairs on the back of my neck. Leans closer and pushes himself against me. And I'm ready to kiss him when I notice the stain on the back of his shirt. A trickle of dots like a chain of islands on a map, colored in red.

Greg's eyes follow mine and he pulls away when he sees that I'm looking at the blood just beneath his shoulder. "This is nothing," he says before I have the chance to ask. "Don't worry, it's not mine." He tells me it happened at practice. One of the guys got scraped up a little. Says it happens all the time and it amazes me sometimes how casual he can be about violence and still be so gentle with me.

"Is he all right?" I ask.

"Yeah, he's fine," Greg says as he stands up. He pulls the stained T-shirt over his head and tosses it to the floor. I've never had any boy undress in front of me and I can't keep from staring. I can see every muscle in his back and chest when he bends to grab another shirt. I think about how easily he could wrap his arms around me and make me vanish.

It sort of frightens me and excites me at the same time. So much so that I sit up, too, and end up standing on the other side of the bed from him as he pulls a clean shirt over his ghost white skin.

I run my finger over the top of his desk, brushing aside pens and pencils and anything that comes across my path. Barely looking at the things I touch, just trying to keep from looking at Greg until my heart slows down.

He walks around the bed. Comes toward me and I take a deep breath. Watching his faint reflection in the glass side of an aquarium perched on the far corner of a bookshelf. I point to it before he has the chance to say anything. "That's not a snake in there, is it?" I demand.

"Nah, it's just a grasshopper," he says, laughing at the disgusted look that crept over my face when I still thought there was a chance he kept a snake only a few feet from his bed.

"*Why* would you have a grasshopper in an aquarium?" I ask, confused but relieved.

"Not just any grasshopper," Greg says. "That grasshopper is undefeated in ten fights."

"Fighting grasshoppers?" I wrinkle my forehead and make my voice higher to let him know I have no idea what he's talking about.

"You've never made grasshoppers fight?" he asks. Showing his surprise by opening his eyes wide when I shake my head. Then he explains how it works. How you hold one in each fist and bring their faces close together. He says the stronger one will end up chewing the other's face to bits.

"That's gross," I say, holding my hand up for him to stop telling me any more about it. He shrugs his shoulders. Says it's no big deal. Tells me that the football team has tournaments every Friday before a game.

I turn my hips away from him because I don't want to hear about it. That's when he puts his hands on my sides and says he's sorry. I feel his words against the back of my neck and feel myself giving in.

Forgiving him.

But later, when we're making out on his bed, I wonder if I'm the only one still thinking about it or if his head is filled with the image of grasshoppers biting each other's faces off, too. And if he is, does it scare him the way it scares me?

# THIRTEEN

After a week of being on the squad, the drama that was swirling around me has gone away as quickly as it came. There're no more rumors circulating the halls about me. I don't get the silent treatment anymore in my classes. Even Morgan and Miranda aren't really enemies anymore. I wouldn't call them best friends or anything like that, but I don't think they hate me, either.

The only person who seems to hate me now is Lukas.

He hasn't talked to me since that night at my house when the sheriff chased him away. I tried to apologize to him. I told him how I swore to the sheriff that he hadn't done anything and how I asked him to leave Lukas alone.

Lukas told me he didn't need my help. Told me to leave him alone as he punched the locker next to mine. From where he was standing, Greg thought he was trying to punch me. He'd heard about what happened at my house and so he was already angry at Lukas. Greg charged at him like I'd seen him charge at opponents on the football field.

I covered my eyes as Lukas's skinny body twisted and bent like the injured bodies strewn over the field during the game he'd taken me to. When I heard him get slammed against the floor, I screamed. I yelled at Greg to get off him. Begged until a teacher rushed into the hall and pulled them apart. Since Lukas is the outcast and Greg's a football player, Lukas was the one to get dragged to the office. I thought about going there and explaining the whole thing, but I knew Lukas would just get angrier at me for interfering.

I tried but I couldn't stay mad at Greg. From what he saw, I guess he was doing the right thing. It was sort of romantic in a brutish jock kind of way. And it only bothered me up till the moment he kissed me there in the hall, in front of everyone. It's strange how the violence that seems to linger on him is always erased whenever our mouths touch.

But even though it's been almost a week, I still can't help feeling bad about me and Lukas. I feel like I let him down. I mean, I sort of did exactly what he said I was going to do the first time we met. I fell in with the Blondes and became one of the popular girls. Now I sit with them at lunch and watch him sitting alone. Every so often, I think I catch him looking at me with the same hateful look I saw in his eyes when he warned me to stay away from Maggie in the first place.

I just wish he'd talk to me so that I could tell him how wrong he was. I'm worried that he's going to drive himself crazy with all his comics and outrageous theories unless I can get through to him. But that doesn't seem likely. I'm pretty sure he never wants to speak to me again.

"God, will you just forget about him already?" Melissa says when she catches me glancing over in the direction of where Lukas is. "What is it with you and that freak? You're going out with one of the hottest boys in school and I still see you looking at him once a day."

"He's not so bad," I say. "Besides, Morgan was friends with him, too, once upon a time," I add in my own defense.

Meredith laughs. "He said that?"

"Yeah, why? It's not true?" I ask.

"Look, you don't have to worry about him anymore," Melissa says. "You're cool now. You can forget about him. Let him disappear into thin air, okay?"

I laugh and try to make it into a joke. "Yeah, I guess. Just an old habit."

"Like chewing your nails?" Meredith asks. Changing the subject to start me on the way to forgetting about him. Grabbing my hand and showing my bitten fingernails to Melissa. "Really, you have to stop that," she says in a friendly enough way.

"I know," I say, taking a closer look and wishing I could stop just like that. Maybe it'll be easier once my dad gets back two days from now. I still get too nervous at night sometimes to quit. It's really before bed that kills me. "I swear that I will soon."

Meredith smiles. "I know you will," she says, less like an encouragement and more like a threat.

It's just part of being one of them, though. They'll always demand that I change something about myself until I'm perfect. It doesn't really get on my nerves. I guess that's because I like who they want me to be more than I like who I am. I mean, they're only trying to make me better. And I'm not so sure conformity is a bad thing in that case. Like my new diet. I only pack a lunch of carrot sticks, yogurt, and bottled water now like the rest of them. It's much healthier than what I ate before. Even if my stomach cramps up with hunger every so often, I know that's only because I was eating too much before. The rest of the girls only eat this much and they have more energy than most two people combined.

My clothes are better, too, now that nearly every girl on the squad has given me old outfits of theirs. Practically new clothes and all of them look great on me. And they've all been really good about not making it feel like charity. None of them has made fun of me for being poor or anything like that. They keep saying that we're family and they don't mind helping out one of their own.

My grades have also gone up.

They always say kids in sports do better in school—I just didn't know that it happened automatically. I don't study any more or anything like that, but I keep getting As on tests. My dad can't wait to see those. He barely believes me when I tell him over the phone.

There's only one thing that kind of makes me feel weird about being one of them. That's the name-change thing. I don't understand why they do it. I mean, not really. I get that it's part of showing allegiance and all that, but it doesn't seem necessary to me.

"Have you decided on one yet?" Maggie asks me.

"Not yet," I mumble, trying to avoid the subject.

"Well, you have to soon. Your first pep rally is Friday and you need a new name by then," she says, making it clear that it's an order. No more stalling, I have to pick one of the three choices she gave me. Montana, Mackenzie, or Madison.

I sigh at the thought of being called by any one of those names. Name changes are for people in the witness protection program, not high school cheerleaders.

"Why is that so important?" I ask.

I regret asking right away as the conversations on either side of the lunch table go silent. All eyes turn to me and then to Maggie, who looks at me coldly. Her blue eyes narrow like the sky before a winter storm. I've seen Maggie get mad at Morgan before or at other girls when they mess up in practice, but she's never given me that icy stare.

"It's just . . . I like my name," I explain.

Maggie blinks and keeps her patience with me. "But your name doesn't begin with an *M* like everyone else's. That's why you need a new one."

"Yeah . . . but I mean, so what?" I ask, almost in a whisper.

" 'So what?' " Maggie whispers back as she leans across the table. Her strawberry lips trembling as she lets the words slip from her mouth slowly so that I don't miss their importance. " 'So what' is that our job is to make sure every single person in this town supports the Death Squad. We need to show how completely loyal we are even if that means giving up part of ourselves. We do that by giving up our names, get it?"

I nod slowly to all the faces staring at me with a serious-
ness that they usually save for practice. "I get it," I say. I get
that it's important to all of them and that should be enough
for it to be important to me, too. "I'll pick one," the syllables scratching the back of my dry throat as I say it.

Maggie smiles at me. She puts her hand on top of mine
and says she knows it might feel strange, but promises me
that I'll get used to it. I'm not so sure about that, but I tell
her I think she's right, anyway.

I go back to eating my lunch and the conversations that
had been cut off start up again without missing a beat. I see
Greg coming over from his table and I wave. All my con-
cerns about changing names go away and I'm beginning to
think I can get used to anything as long as I have him.

I let my hand slide slowly down the side of Greg's cheek after
our mouths give each other space to breathe.

"See you tomorrow," I say.

"Yeah. Tomorrow," Greg says. His face switching from
pink to pale as the diner sign flickers on and off above his
head. Some of his friends are still inside and I can see them
in their varsity jackets, shuffling from table to table like children playing musical chairs.

Our fingertips linger together for a second before slipping apart. I start to walk away, still facing him. I take careful, backward steps until I'm in front of the building next to
the diner. I wave one last time and he waves back and I already miss his closeness.

The town is deserted as I move through it like a shadow.

The stores have all closed for the night and the lights have been turned off behind their large shop windows. The wind picks up as I walk. I look once over my shoulder and see Greg is still there, watching me as I turn the corner. The thought of him will keep me warm as I make my way home. It's a little scary sometimes the way he can make me feel. So nervous and safe at the same time. So completely his, like a stuffed animal that loves being loved. I don't know what it is exactly. I only know that I like it. That I like being around him.

The days have dwindled down to nothing with the approach of winter. The purple sky of evening is fading quickly and I know it won't last me the whole way home. Even as I hurry my steps, night is already moving in to take over. The streetlights glow brighter. The space between growing blacker. The creaking of the tree trunks swaying in the wind getting louder. The loneliness of the world around me makes it easy to drift away.

I count silently in my head. Counting out the rhythm of the routines I'm supposed to do tomorrow at the pep rally. It'll be my first time in front of a crowd and I'm starting to get nervous that I'm going to screw up. I've nailed each of them in practice the last few days, but it's different when there are people watching. I know most of them will be watching me, too. Fixed on me, waiting to see if I belong. The rest of the girls will be, too, to an extent. They might not say it in so many words, but I know tomorrow is going to be my final test.

I go through the steps in my head as I walk. Tapping my feet and keeping my eyes rolled back as my mouth moves, "One. Two. Three. And one . . ." Starting over each time I forget a movement here or a gesture there. I'm so distracted by it that I don't notice the figure lurking by the bushes near my house until I'm too close to run away.

A small scream escapes me like the sound of a dog yelping as shadow arms and legs move out from behind the cover of shrubs. A scream that I cut short and swallow back down once I notice it's only Lukas.

"What are you doing here?" I ask once my heart stops racing from the shock. I catch my breath and smile. I don't care so much that he startled me, I'm just glad to see him.

He doesn't say anything at first. He stands there silently in my driveway, his sneakers trampling the oil stain that has faded in the last ten days. Tilts his head to the side to shake away the loose strands of hair hanging in front of his eyes so he can get a better look at me. I realize then that it's the first time he's seen me in my cheerleader uniform and it kind of freaks him out a little.

I pull the ends of my coat together to hide.

Lukas shakes his head and gives me a disgusted laugh. It's the last straw and I push past him. I don't need him to come by here and judge me. Who does he think he is, anyway?

"Hannah, wait," he says, trying to sound nice.

"Screw you!" I shout and keep marching toward the door.

"I'm sorry," he says. "Just wait a minute . . . let me talk to you."

"Why should I?" I ask. "I've tried to talk to you for a week and you treat me like I'm a disease." I fumble through my pocket for my house key. I take it out, slip it in the lock, and the door clicks open.

"I know," he says. There's something sad in his voice that

makes me pause. "I've been kind of a jerk." Then he looks at me with the same gentle eyes he looked at me the night my dad pulled away. I think about how he stayed with me for hours in the cold that night so that I wouldn't have to be alone. The least I can do is stand out here for a few minutes and listen to what he has to say.

I pull the door closed again and put my keys back in my pocket. Sitting down on the steps, I fold my hands in my lap. He comes closer to me, leans against the pole but won't sit down. Takes a deep breath and I can almost see him trying to put the words together in his head before he speaks.

"You have to quit."

He says it as simple as that. Without any explanation. Without a reason. Without even considering how I might respond.

My response is to spring back to my feet and open the door again.

"Wait, listen to me," he begs.

"I've listened to it all before, I'm not going to listen to it again."

"Here! Look," he shouts. He slips his arms through the straps of his backpack and lets it slide off his shoulders. He searches in the dark, rummaging through the papers like an animal digging in a trash bin for something worth eating before he pulls out a photograph with torn edges and creases running down the middle. He smooths it over with his palm, uncurls the corners, and flattens it out on his leg before handing it to me.

"What's this?" I ask, not making any attempt to take the picture.

He doesn't answer me, just shoves the photograph into my hand.

It's hard to see anything at all so I reach inside and switch on the porch light. The image of two people comes into focus in the glare of electricity. I can tell right away that the one figure is Lukas. He looks a little different. Younger, but still long and thin and the same crooked smile that I'm used to. The person next to him is a girl that I've never seen before. He has his arm around her and she's smiling, too. They are standing on the street that runs behind our school but it takes me a minute to recognize it because the houses in the background are brightly painted and I'm used to seeing them empty and gray with boards in the windows. I can't imagine Maplecrest ever looking that alive.

I hand the picture back to him, holding my arms out to my sides to ask him what the point was of showing it to me.

"That's me and Alison two years ago," Lukas says.

I don't believe him at first. The girl didn't look anything like Morgan. She had brown hair and her eyes didn't melt through the paper like blue flames the way I would expect them to. Besides, Meredith told me that was all a lie. That Lukas had made the whole thing up for some reason.

I bring the picture back up in the light and take another look. A faint resemblance starts to show this time, but in a strange way. It's almost like I can see Morgan trapped underneath the surface. I get the feeling if I took an eraser and ran it over the face in the photograph and blew away the dust, I'd see Morgan staring back at me. One layer below this face and one layer above the skeleton.

Lukas can read the surprise in my expression.

"The same thing's going to happen to you," he says.

"I doubt it," I say. Trying to convince myself more than him. Trying to tell myself that the shivering fit that runs from my hips down to my ankles is only from the cold gust of air getting under my skirt and that it has nothing to do with the bone-thin image of myself that floats behind my eyelids.

The long branches of the pine trees shake and rustle as the wind blows over the hills behind my house. The beams that hold up the ceiling creak as the roof moans under the strain. It's like a song of death that shatters my words and leaves them like so many pieces of broken glass to be blown down the abandoned street.

Lukas's face takes on the features of the night as he stares at me like a messenger transformed into the bad news he's come to bring me. "I know you don't want to believe me . . . but there's something really messed up that's happening here," he says. "People go missing and no one seems to notice. People change overnight and have no memory of who they were and everyone else just goes on acting like nothing's wrong!"

I cover my face with my hands to ignore him. Press my fingers into my eye sockets until purple and green circles appear. I use them to block out the memory of hypnotized eyes in the crowd at the football game. Pushing away the broken furniture in Diana's house and remembering how no one missed her, almost like they knew it was going to happen. And floating behind everything that races through my mind are the mirrored glasses of the sheriff that keep anyone from seeing his soul.

"Think about it, Hannah . . . you know I'm right," Lukas says.

"No . . . no . . . you're just imagining it," I say, shaking my head.

"No . . . I'm not," he says as calmly as the waitress at the diner might when taking an order for coffee. Not arguing. Not questioning. Simply telling me a fact that he has come to know. "I know you have your new friends and all . . . a boyfriend and everything . . . I didn't really expect you to listen to me."

"Then why did you come here?" I ask.

He hands me the photograph again and makes me take it. "I wanted to give you that," he says. "If there's anything left of you when they're done, I figure this might help you re-member me. Once you're one of them, they're going to get rid of me. Once there's no chance of you caring."

"What does that mean?"

"It means I kept my mouth shut after Alison, just like everyone else does, but this time I didn't and they're going to make sure I don't spoil their plans for anyone else," he says.

The way he says it is like saying good-bye forever. I try to tell him how crazy all this is, but he won't listen. Tells me again that he knows he's the next one who will go missing. Says as soon as I'm one of them, they'll come after him.

He turns the collar of his coat up to the wind and steps off the porch. I don't know if I want to stop him and make him come inside with me, or if I want to run after him and shove him to the ground until he tumbles down the driveway.

I'm so confused about everything that I just stand there with the tattered picture between my fingers as Lukas starts around the side of my house to cut through the woods. I see him illuminated and clear for a second as a pair of high beams crisscross the yard just as he disappears into the cover of trees.

I turn away just in time to see a pair of static blue eyes watching me through the window as the police car slowly cruises to the end of my street and turns toward town.

My hands are numb from the cold. My knees are shaking, too, but I don't think it has anything to do with the wind. Part of me wants to take off in the direction of town and find Greg, throw my arms around him, and make him hold me until I'm sure everything is okay. Until I know nothing is any different from how it appears.

The phone stops me, though. Its ringing is like an alarm clock that wakes me out of a dream and I rush into the house, bolting the door behind me. My hand's still shaking when I answer the phone and I'm afraid my voice gives it away.

My dad asks if everything's okay.

"Just hurry home," I tell him.

# FOURTEEN

Okay...Madison it is, then," Maggie says after I've told her which of the selected names I prefer. She smiles like a kid wanting to show off a trophy she's just won, her teeth glowing like bleached bones in the fluorescent lights of the school hallways. "Madison," she repeats to herself, considering it carefully one last time before draping it over me like a necklace that can never be taken off.

I close my locker and wish I could feel even a fraction of the enthusiasm she has about my new name. It feels like a pair of jeans that will never fit me. The whole idea of it makes me restless. It's like the photograph of Morgan, like the first layer has just been erased and it won't take long until I'm exactly the same.

I try to tell myself it's just my nerves as we start walking toward the gym. We have to get changed into our uniforms before the pep rally begins and I'm terrified that I'm going to mess up. Even so, I know it's more than that. I'd gotten so caught up with fitting in that I hadn't really stopped to think how it was changing me. Being called by a different name has a way of putting it all into perspective pretty quickly.

I've been ignoring things on purpose.

I've been refusing to see how different events are connected. I should've known better. There are no coincidences in small towns. Things are always connected. That's what Lukas was trying to make me realize in his own insane way. But what things are connected to which? That's what I need to figure out now. Like figuring out if Diana's going missing has anything to do with the sheriff keeping an eye on my house? Or maybe he keeps driving by because of my dad, getting ready to harass us like other small-town cops we've met. And more important, does any of that have anything to do with me being a cheerleader at Maplecrest High with a new name?

I'm not even sure I want to know. Being ignorant of things can be nice sometimes. But I know the photograph of Alison tucked away in my bedroom will haunt me if I don't try to find out. I don't want Madison to kill Hannah the way Morgan killed Alison. So I take a deep breath through my nose and get my courage up. "Maggie . . . there's something I've wanted to ask you," I say as the kids move out of our way to let us pass through the center of the hall.

"Sure, Madison, what is it?" Maggie says.

It surprises me how quickly she's adopted my new name. It sounds so natural, like she's never called me by anything else. So matter of fact that it throws me off and I forget the words I was going to say.

"Well?" she asks impatiently as we turn the corner.

I put my hands near my mouth, fighting off the urge to chew my nails in order to avoid a lecture from Maggie about my bad habits. "I . . . um," I stutter, not sure if I should let it go and just concentrate on the routines. The whole thing is stupid, anyway. It's from being alone for ten days. I start to make up things and go a little crazy. I just need to push it out of my mind. I nearly convince myself, but then she looks at me with those deep blue eyes like the ones that cut through the darkness last night and I know I need to ask.

"Your dad . . . I saw him last night driving by my house." The way I say it is like an accusation. Lets her know that I think there's something weird about it. And Maggie just looks at me like I'm a little kid, tells me that he *is* the sheriff, and that *is* his job. Then she gives me the look I've seen her give a thousand times whenever someone messes up at practice or says the wrong thing in the lunchroom. One raised eyebrow and her mouth slightly open. The look that makes whoever she's looking at feel like the dumbest person on earth.

"But there was another time, too," I tell her, referring to the time he happened to be there to throw Lukas to the ground. And I think there's been more than just one other time. I think it was his headlights and not anyone looking for my dad that kept me up the first few nights after my dad left. "I was just wondering . . . I mean, has he said anything about it?"

I feel Maggie's fingers wrap around my wrist, gripping me tightly like an angry bird of prey. I turn to look at her, wondering what I did that was so wrong, that made her snap. But her expression doesn't match the viciousness of her fingernails making little marks in my skin. She's smiling and friendly and it doesn't fit. Like when the soundtrack to a movie is off and the lips don't match up with the dialogue. I keep looking back and forth from her hand squeezing my arm to her face. She must realize how strange it seems, too, because she lets go, pulling her hand back like someone letting go of a power line after getting a shock.

She takes a deep breath and breathes it out slowly, like getting herself ready to spill a secret she didn't want to tell me. Leans in closer and whispers out of the hearing of those around us in the crowded hallway. "We know your dad's out of town," she confesses.

My eyes grow wider than my face has room for, giving away the lie I'm telling by shaking my head. My mouth makes up the same lies, saying how my dad just works strange hours because I know what it means if Maggie's dad finds out. A long line of court appointments and weekend stays at foster care until things get sorted out.

"It's okay," Maggie assures me. She puts one hand on each shoulder to get me to relax. "My dad's not going to get you into any trouble or anything. He was just checking up on you to make sure you were safe . . . you know, because of that freak kid who attacked you and everything."

I tuck my lower lip under my teeth.

It should make me feel better, but it doesn't. Makes me feel like I'm being watched. Studied. The same way Meredith watches me to make sure I lose all my old habits. Maggie can tell, too. She can always tell. She sees that it hasn't relaxed me at all, so she locks her elbow with mine and playfully nudges me in the side. "Hey, you still in there?" she says and I nod, not really in the mood. But then she makes her voice serious again, telling me that it's only because they care about me. "You don't have to be alone ever again," she says.

I look for any sign that she's teasing me. Listening for the slightest crack in her voice or the tiniest start of a laugh. Stare into her eyes to see if they are hiding any kind of contempt for me, but they are clear and open and I know she's being genuine. She really cares about me and here I am, leaping to conclusions about her dad. "I'm sorry . . . I was . . . ," but I don't finish, because I'm not sure anything I say will come out right.

"Whatever, don't worry about it," Maggie says, making me feel worse by being so understanding. "Come on, let's get ready and forget about all this."

"Yeah, okay," I agree. I feel so dumb for letting a bunch of ghost stories and bad dreams make me paranoid. Like I didn't have enough to stress about. In twenty minutes I'm going to be in front of the entire school performing for the first time in my life. That's the thing that should really be making my stomach toss and turn as we walk into the locker room.

Most of the other girls are already dressed in their uniforms and gossiping when Maggie raises her voice above the chatter to get their attention. The conversations trail off like the breaking apart of an airplane's exhaust cloud across the sky. Once they're all staring at us, she reaches over and brushes the hair away from my face, tucking it behind my ear. "Everybody, this is Madison."

My heart thumps sharply against the inside of my ribs.

A sad, sudden good-bye to Hannah as I'm one step closer to not being me.

Another layer eroded away. But it's not all as terrible as I thought because it's also another layer that separates me from my friends vanishing. And I can see it now that they're all happy. All these girls who terrified me two weeks ago with their intimidating eyes and beautiful features, they are now my friends. Even the few of them who still don't particularly want me here would stand up for me if it came down to picking sides between me and anyone else. That's more than I can say for most of the kids at a lot of other schools who claimed to like me a lot.

"Hi," I say, keeping my hand down by my hip and waving with just my fingers. Waving as Madison for the first time and I think maybe I might grow into it after all.

"Okay, let's get ready! Showtime in fifteen minutes, girls!" Mrs. Donner's voice shouts from the doorway leading into the gym. We can hear the marching, charging footsteps of the school filing into the bleachers in the background. I feel my heart start to race, pounding in rhythm with the gathering crowd.

Lockers open and close all around me like a chorus of crashing cars. Meredith comes over and sits on the bench next to me. "Nervous, huh?" she says with her hands calmly folded and resting in the pleats of her skirt.

"A little," I say sarcastically, holding my thumb and finger an inch apart.

Meredith laughs the easy way she always does and tells me, "Don't be."

"Thanks for the advice," I say and we both laugh. Surprisingly, though, it helps. Being able to laugh kind of pushes the worry aside as I change out of my clothes and into my uniform.

"You look perfect," she says.

I put my head down and look myself over. I guess I'd been so focused at practice that I didn't notice before, but the uniform isn't too tight anymore. Meredith is right, it fits me perfectly. I'm still not as thin as Miranda or Melissa, or anyone else, but if I look closely, I can see the bones of my hips waiting just under the surface to show through like twigs.

Meredith stands up and tilts my head up so that I'm facing her. "Finishing touches," she says and I close my eyes so that she can apply my makeup. All the girls have painted their strawberry lips with a more violent candy-red lipstick. I pretend to blow a kiss and Meredith smears the color over me. Powders my skin to the same ghostly shade as hers and draws heavy black lines around my eyes.

I catch a glimpse of myself in the mirror when she's done.

The only way I can tell myself from everyone else is the shade of my hair.


The principal's voice drones on behind me as I stand facing the kids stacked on the gym bleachers. I'm only half listening as he speaks over the microphone. He sounds like a robot, stiff and monotone as he welcomes the entire school into the gym. His words float up to the rafters to die among the state championship banners that hang there, dusty old accomplishments with faded letters alongside new ones declaring our school's superiority in vivid bloodred letters.

I take brief glances over my shoulder to look at the football team. They're seated in the middle of the gym in chairs that have been set up specifically for them. I try to find Greg somewhere among the nearly identical faces. I guess I didn't notice before how alike they all look. The football players, I mean. I'm only used to seeing them in small groups, or wearing helmets and numbers. Then I can always tell Greg apart from the rest—he's the one always looking at me. I can't pick him out in a large group like this, though. Can't find his smile when I really need him. I need to see him smile at me just once because the nervous sickness in my stomach is starting to swell as the pep rally gets going.

One look from Greg would settle me down. His eyes have a way of calming me, like the sky does, or a lake, or anything else that's soft and blue. I could use a little of that. I could use some calm as the circus begins to unfold around me.

"Pssst . . . turn around," Miranda hisses when she spies me looking away from the crowd. "Now!" she demands through clenched teeth.

I snap my head around and face forward.

I'm supposed to keep my eyes on the kids in the bleachers. After we came out of the locker room and performed a quick routine, Mrs. Donner assigned us each to a section. A cheerleader standing at attention every few feet apart, all around the gym, watching the watchers. No one mentioned it to me before, but judging from the reaction of the other girls, it's obvious that's our job in the pep rally ceremony.

We're supposed to make sure everyone pays attention.

We're supposed to remember those who don't cheer when they are supposed to. Anyone talking while they're supposed to be listening. Anyone passing notes or doing homework. Anyone at all who doesn't watch in fixed silence like statues.

We are the prison guards and it makes most of the girls giddy.

We enforce school spirit and they take it very seriously.

The other kids know it, too. They stare at me with blank looks. Their hands stay quietly in their laps until it's time for them to applaud. Scheduled applause signaled by Maggie each time she raises her arm as she stands on the podium next to the principal. Afraid not to because they know what happens when they don't. So do I only after the first time Miranda notices a lethargic spectator and whispers to me.

"Him? See him?" she asks, pointing to a sleepy-eyed freshman with his head resting in his hands when he should be clapping. I point him out, too, as if to ask if that's the kid she's talking about. She nods. Her face twisted into the face of an angry dog as she looks over to the teachers standing by each door to make sure no one leaves. Getting their attention, Miranda points at the boy again whose eyes are heavy and hasn't noticed he's in trouble.

One of the teachers comes over immediately. A hairy-knuckled gym teacher with the face of an ape. He barrels his way through the bleachers. Students dodging him as he plows through, grabs the sleepy-eyed runt, and drags him down by the collar. The kid's arms swing to keep his balance with the *thump-thump* of his sneakers hitting against each step. He tries to speak but it comes out all garbled in fear as the seated kids move aside without a word of protest to let them pass.

My knees begin to shake as the gym teacher pulls the boy outside and disappears in the glare of the sun. And I'm sure I must have missed something. The tired look on the kid's face must have been a cover-up to hide some more inappropriate act that Miranda saw. "They'd never take him out like that for nothing," I tell myself again and again.

The principal continues his speech without taking any notice. Introducing the football players. "Our deliverers of death," he says in a spitting voice of madness. I figure if I could just see his face, I'd see a hint of humor that I can't hear. With my back turned, it all sounds like the ravings of a preacher my dad and I saw on the street corner once in Boston. A sermon of hatred that he delivered with a drooling rage. His suit and tie and neatly trimmed hair all transform into the picture of a wild beast with a split tongue and sharp red eyes. That's the same way I see the principal in my mind as he reads their names one by one, starting with the seniors. I don't dare look until he gets to the juniors and feel relieved that the principal still looks like the same mild-mannered bore that he always is and that only his voice has changed.

I wait for Greg's name to be called, peeking sideways out of the corner of my eye and making sure Miranda isn't watching me. I turn around and see him rising above the other boys sitting around him. There's something different about him that I don't recognize. Something more violent. The bones in his skull show through the thin layer of his face. His eyes are sunken and the skin around them looks itchy and irritated like a rash. A manipulated roar erupts from the crowd and Greg shows them a demon face that I've never seen.

It freezes my blood and I quickly turn around.

It's for the show. Pretend toughness and everything. It shouldn't bother me. It's part of him being a jock. Part of what I have to learn to deal with. Like the grasshoppers and poor table manners. But with everything else, it's all just a little much to take in at once as I return to my position. This just isn't what I expected. None of it. I thought the kids would stare at me in awe, but they only stare at me in fear.

After the introductions, the football coach speaks to the school. He walks around the gym and doesn't use the microphone. Shouting in a voice bigger than I thought could come out of such a short person. Shorter than the players, but he roars like someone twice as tall. The veins in his forehead stick out and his face turns fiery red as he talks about the opponent. "This isn't about a game," he says. "This is about a way of life. Our way of life! And if they think they can come into our town and try to kick that out of us, they got something to learn."

His players respond like soldiers chanting after a drill sergeant as the coach makes the game sound less like a game with each thing he says. He makes it sound like a war against enemies too menacing to show mercy to. Line after line, he gets more animated, pounding his fists against chairs, tables, and whatever else is in his path. I can feel the floorboards vibrate under my feet after each round of thunderous applause from the bleachers. But it's like their bodies are going through the motions, stomping their feet and yelling, but I can see in their eyes they don't feel anything.

Every inch of my skin is begging me to run away, but I fight it. Keep my hands on my hips and my elbows bent like I'm supposed to. Keep searching row after row of vacant faces. And the more the coach yells, the more I feel like I'm trapped in a dream waiting for a tree to shoot up through the floor. Waiting to be tied to the trunk and have my insides chewed out by ravenous razor teeth. And the more I think about it, the more things begin to spin. The banners hanging in the rafters blur into a tornado of letters and the faces in front of me swirl around until I can't make out one from the next, getting dizzier and beginning to panic that I'm going to faint.

I place the back of my hand on my forehead. My hair is drenched with sweat but my skin is cold to the touch. I take deep breaths and try to pull myself together. On the other side of me, Mandy keeps whispering in my direction and asking if I'm okay. Her voice sounds like the slow leak from a tire and getting distant, but I nod anyway.

"Fine," I mouth back to her.

The blood flowing through my temples begins to pound with each booming syllable echoing off the high ceilings. The words feel like insects trying to crawl into my ears. Stinging and buzzing. And once they burrow in, I will be as dead as the bodies piled high into the bleachers in front of me. Rewired and reborn and I can't do anything to stop it.

Squinting my eyes shut doesn't turn it off.

Neither does pressing my fingers against the side of my head.

"Madison? Are you all right?" I can hear the voice say but it sounds distorted. Sounds like it's being spoken underwater but getting closer.

I feel a pair of arms wrap around my waist just as the world flashes into white light like stars exploding as I pass out.

Through the windows, everything looks the way it's supposed to. Everything looks quiet like the world has gone to sleep as the clouds break apart in the first snow of the year. I see the flakes coming down in the sliver of glass that wraps around the walls in the locker room just under the roof. So calm and perfect. A steady rain of large flakes, the kind that are good for building snowmen but are bad for sledding. Clean white snow like the skin of those standing above me as I lie on the bench and blink my eyes.

I try to sit up, but I'm not as ready as I thought. All the blood rushes to my head and someone takes hold of me from behind, lowering me back down. My eyes adjust to the light and things come into focus. I can see Meredith standing next to me, her hands behind her back and leaning slightly to the side as her foot taps slow and steady like the snow falling outside. She looks like a ceramic figure, a toy left out for attention. Morgan is whispering in her ear. Her hands moving as she speaks but there are no words. None that I can hear anyway and it's like watching television with the sound turned off.

It will come back, though.

Slowly the way seeing does when I blink.

From the looks on the faces towering over me, I'm not so sure I want it to return. I'm sure when I do, the first thing I'll be told is that I'm off the squad. I must be such an embarrassment to them, fainting in front of the entire school like that. Some impression I made—I bet the bored spectators woke up then. I'm sure they didn't have to fake their laughter. I doubt Greg will ever talk to me again, either. Not after I ruined the pep rally, bringing it to a sudden end when I crashed to the floor.

"She's such a waste of time," the words making their way from Morgan's mouth and drifting down to me. Maggie is standing next to her now, in front of her, arms crossed and eyes peering at me. "I told you we should've just gotten rid of her." Morgan smirks, proud of the fact she'd known all along that I was worthless.

Maggie tosses her hair over her shoulder and glances at Morgan. Shutting her up with the look she saves to remind us all that we were nothing until the day she first talked to us. That we were no one until she named us. When she turns back to face me, the look grows stronger, like it's been building inside her, just waiting for me to make a mistake. Waiting to lash out at me for not being as perfect as the rest of her clones.

I want to say I'm sorry, but the words don't come out of me. They get stuck somewhere inside and I'm afraid to say them. Afraid they'll only make things worse as Maggie kneels down and places one hand over mine and the other on my forehead so that I can't lift my head. Trapped like an animal caught in wire jaws. And when she smiles, she's letting me know that she owns me completely.

"What happened out there, Madison?" she asks like a school nurse does when she thinks you're faking an illness to get out of class. Commanding me to talk like I'm a pet. Her least favorite pet and she wants me to know it.

"Nothing," I whisper, feeling ready to cry.

I wish the snow could fall so fast that it covered up the last two weeks and I could start over once it melted. If I could go back, I wouldn't have starved myself for days and gotten so weak that I started hallucinating and passed out. Maybe I never would have tried out, either. It's the stress of trying to fit in that's made me so on edge lately. Made my senses distort reality and imagine things that can't be true.

Maggie's fingers begin to move through my hair like the legs of a spider. She makes her voice into a soothing sound the way people do when trying to get an infant to stop squealing. And when I finally feel brave enough to look her in the eye, it's comforting to see she's not angry. "It could happen to anyone," she says and I see Morgan roll her eyes and put her hands on her hips, disappointed at my being given a second chance to make things right.

I start to tell Maggie that I don't know what came over me, that I just got overwhelmed and nervous, but Maggie puts her hand in front of my mouth. She tells me it's okay. "As long as you promise it won't happen during the game tomorrow," she says with a laugh that is echoed by the other girls.

"But . . . am I still on the squad?" I ask.

The mood in the locker room changes the instant the words come out.

"No one ever gets thrown off the squad once you're on," Meredith explains to me.

"Nothing you did was so bad that it can't be fixed," Maggie says. "The pep rally was almost over, anyway. And besides, it's kind of boring listening to the same stupid speeches every time."

"Yeah?" I ask. They seemed so serious that I never thought they'd think that way, too. But my perception has been off lately. And I guess I'm not so different from the rest of them because Maggie assures me that they can't stand listening to the principal and Mr. Johnson, the football coach, any more than I could. To prove it, she curls her hands into fists and begins imitating the coach by grunting and foaming at the mouth in an exaggerated impersonation.

I start to feel better as I begin to laugh. My headache fades and I feel strong enough to sit up. Maybe fainting wasn't such a big deal after all. I mean, if I think about it, probably no one was laughing at me over it. They're probably more worried that I'm hurt or something. And anyway, the school day ended ten minutes early because of it. I'm probably a hero to some of them.

"Feeling better?" Maggie asks and I smile. I tell her I can't believe I did that, but that I'm fine now. "Good," she says, "because we've got something we need to do."

The other girls move in closer, too excited to keep still. I move my eyes back and forth and bite my lip trying to figure out what Maggie's hinting about. The sun breaks through the clouds for a brief moment, making a tiny halo appear above her golden hair and it dawns on me even before Maggie says it.

"We've got to bleach your hair before tomorrow so that you'll be as perfect as the rest of us," she says, taking a few loose strands of my straw-colored hair in her hand and twisting them into the light where they don't sparkle the way hers does. It will, though. Soon enough, it will.

# FIFTEEN

My vision is reduced to tiny slits just below the blindfold and I can barely make out the red *M* tattooed on the chest of my uniform in the dim light. I keep my head down and my eyes focused on it to keep my mind off the parade of hands tugging and pulling me forward. I slide my feet over the floor, trying not to stumble as I'm dragged through the maze of benches and lockers.

"Can't I take this off?" I ask the voices that float around me like so much static on the radio when the stations go in and out of range.

"I told you, you have to wear it," Maggie says from somewhere in front of me, somewhere in the darkness. "It'll keep the bleach from getting in your eyes." But if it's such a safety precaution, I wonder why they didn't wait until we were in the other room before tying the shadows over my eyes, instead of already doing it while I was on the bench.

I try to manage my steps, try to keep pace and not trip over the feet of those leading me to the equipment room where they say is the best place to dye my hair because there's a sink and a chair and everything we need to make me as blond as the winter sunshine.

The deadbolt clicks and I hear the heavy door creak open inches away. The sour, rotting smell of dead mice seeps into my nostrils and my stomach turns over. Four hands clutch at each of my arms and pull me to the source of the odor. I hesitate and they pull harder. "It's really nasty," I protest, struggling to get my hands free so that I can cover my mouth and nose to keep from gagging.

"Don't be so stupid," Morgan says. "The bleach will kill the smell in a second." She gives me a little shove as she finishes speaking and I fall back into an invisible chair placed there to catch me. There's a rustling through boxes and the shuffling of feet around me and I try to peek by rubbing my shoulder against the blindfold to push it up and let more of the room into view.

Someone grabs the loose ends of the scarf, pulls my head back like yanking a dog's leash to keep it away from something it's not supposed to get into. Then the last remaining light is sealed off when the knot is cinched tighter at the back of my head.

I can sense the figures moving around me like ghosts moving behind the walls of my house at night. My breathing grows quick and scattered at the clattering sound of glass and the silence of my friends. I only hear the whispering rise and fall of their lungs when they exhale. The whistling air sounds like a pit of snakes hissing with pointed tongues.

"Maybe I shouldn't do this," I say, sounding as worried as I can.

"Don't be scared," Meredith's familiar voice says close to my ear.

"I'm not," I lie. "It's just, you know, I should make sure it's okay with my dad first." They tell me not to be such a child. That it's no big deal. But I keep arguing with them because something doesn't feel right. Nothing has felt right all day and I make up my mind to start listening to my instincts.

I go to stand up but I'm quickly pushed back down. Pinned to the chair and held tight by a series of hands holding my elbows and wrists. Warm breath on my cheek as someone slithers in close, putting her knee into my stomach as she speaks. "Maybe you'd like it better if I had my dad take you away to a foster home," Maggie says.

I can tell by the way she says it that it's not just a threat. She'd actually go through with it. And for the first time since meeting her, I know exactly how mean she can be.

I swallow any fight I have left in me and shut up.

"Slide the chair over and lean her head back into the sink," Maggie orders once she's released me. The instructions are carried out immediately. The screeching scrape of metal against the floor fills the room. My head makes a dull noise when it hits against the base of the sink. Then nothing, as if everyone else has evaporated and left only the low swishing of socks sweeping across the floor.

Waiting for whatever is supposed to happen next makes me feel sick to my stomach. I want to get out of the chair and scream at them all to stop, but it's like I don't have a tongue and I don't have limbs. And I'm blind to the shadows that crawl like animals around their kill. The dream sensation of teeth chewing open my skin creeps along my spine at the touch of fingernails scratching lightly against my scalp.

I don't expect it when the warm water suddenly soaks my hair. No sound of running faucets to get me prepared and I have to bite my tongue to keep from screaming out. It burns like gasoline against my skin and I figure out that it's not water at all but bleach, melting the color from each strand of hair to be washed down the drain.

There's a moment then when nobody's hands are holding me down and I know it's my only chance. I tell myself that if I could see what's going on, it wouldn't be so bad. I reach up and dig my fingers under the blindfold and pull it up over my eyes. I see Morgan make a desperate attempt to stop me, but by the time she grabs hold of my wrist and bends it back it's too late.

I see everything.

The metal shelves against the wall, stacked with countless glass jars that shimmer like rubies in the flickering fluorescent light. Filled with heavy red water, only thicker. Each has a strip of masking tape across the front with a name written in black marker. Names I know. Names that begin with the same letter. Hundreds of them, from floor to ceiling like books in a library.

I don't realize what they are until I see the one in Meredith's pale hands. The fresh smell of Magic Marker chemicals still lingers where my fake name has been scrawled onto the label. Madison. And I notice that it isn't a jar at all, but more like the containers in a hospital that connect to tubes and drain into the patient.

I am the patient.

The blood in the jar is supposed to go inside of me.

It's supposed to go inside me the same way other jars are going inside Miranda and Melissa in the far corner of the room. Lying down on cots with their eyes rolled back in their heads and only the white parts showing beneath pink eyelids. Plastic tubes stuck in their arms and sucking out the liquid like straws where it will run blue through their veins.

I make a noise to talk but nothing comes out.

"Sit back," Morgan shouts. She's holding my wrist so tightly that she cuts off the circulation. I can feel my fingers going numb. I can see the skin turning white like the pavement in the snowstorm. White like them. White like a zombie with someone else's blood to keep them alive.

I see it all now the way I should have seen it before. See it in the electric stare of dead eyes. The snarl of chapped lips that reveal sharp teeth for biting through bones. Death chants and disappearances. The pale skin of corpses that try to hide under makeup. But they can't hide anymore. Not once they see that I figured it out. It's like a switch turns on inside them.

The pupils of their eyes start to glow like rust through the electric blue.

A series of rashes breaks out on their perfect porcelain skin.

Their pretty faces have become distorted masks like in my nightmares.

"No . . . no . . . no," I stutter, not able to really speak

clearly or even think clearly as I struggle to stand up. Morgan lashes toward me with her mouth open and her hands held like claws. So fast like blurry images sped up on a movie screen. Slicing through the plastic chair with a swipe of her hands. A laceration in the fabric where my face had been an instant before.

They all reach for me then, but I manage to get through the grasp of their dead arms laced with spider veins that show through more when they're angry. Communicating with one another by growling and snarling instead of words as I rush for the door. Grabbing at the handle in a panic, my fingers slip. Slip again and I start to scream as they start to get closer because I know if I don't get out before they capture me that I won't come out alive. I won't come out until I'm like them.

Meredith drops the jar in her hands to the floor and the shattering glass breaks like rain. Blood splatters against my leg and I stare for a split second too long. Long enough for Meredith to grab my arm and twist it behind my back in a sudden shot of pain.

"You're not leaving," she growls in a heavy voice. The air escapes my lungs in a weak gasp of breath when she slams me against the wall. I feel the heat from her mouth on my skin. The stench of old rotting wounds makes me gag as she breathes on me. Twisting my arm like a twig that's ready to snap. "You're either one of us or you're one of them."

Pushing me harder against the wall and crushing the bones in my face. My cheek pressed against a piece of paper, smearing onto my skin the ink of names that are crossed off.

The last name on the list is Diana's. A thin red line runs through the letters and makes me shudder because I know what it means without having to be told.

They killed her.

They killed everyone.

The blood inside them is the blood stolen from empty houses. Rejected people reused and reborn into them. That's what she means by one of them. Part of the blood supply.

Lukas was right. He was right about everything. Maplecrest isn't a ghost town. It's a graveyard.

Vomit tickles the back of my throat as I shout for Meredith to leave me alone. Begging her because I know now that this is how they do it. This is how they plan to make me one of them. By infecting me with diseased blood so that I can help them kill. So that I will tear apart the others and feed off their flesh until the entire town is rid of anyone who isn't like them.

"Please," I beg. Repeating the word over and over until it gets broken up in my mouth and comes out only as tears. Saying it until it becomes too weak to mean anything.

Maggie approaches. Slow and careful because she's hunting me. Running her tongue over her teeth like an animal ready to feed. And when she speaks, it's not with her voice but with the guttural voice of someone being strangled. The voice of hatred. The voice of murder when she says I'm only good for spare parts now.

My heart thumps like a caged bird inside my ribs. Screaming through my veins to flee. To fight. To run. To do whatever I need to do to get away because I don't want to die. I manage to grab on to the metal shelf beside me with my free hand. I ignore the pain running through the arm pinned between my shoulder blades and pull as hard as I can.

Meredith lets go of me in horror as the shelf creaks and begins to tilt. The sharp pain in my elbow and shoulder fade to an ache when she releases me and tries to keep the shelves from toppling before all the containers are spilled.

The rest of them rush to help her, too, because the blood is more important than I am. The blood is what keeps them pretty. The blood is what keeps them from being just a rotting corpse that can't die. It is also what is going to save my life.

I rush out into the locker room as a chorus of broken glass fills the air behind me like the sound of gunshots. And the same thing is happening to the girls who were waiting outside to see my transformation. Their pretty complexions rotting away before my eyes as they growl like dogs when I push past them.

They're slow to react and I manage to make it into the hallway. I yell for someone, anyone to come help me. But I'm really yelling for Greg. Running to the boys' locker room and calling him by name now.

It's not him who opens the door. It's not a him at all but one of them. A zombie with rust stains around electric blue eyes like the cheerleaders only bigger. Stronger. More aggressive and I wonder if they have Greg, too. Wonder if they've always had him, if he's been in disguise the whole time as I run past the gym and head for the exit. And I know the inhuman cry that echoes from the school behind me is the sound of my death sentence.

**The snowflakes fall** like slow-motion static on the television, suspended in the air for a moment before falling. So beautiful as I run through them that if I let myself, I could almost forget the horror that surrounds me. The horror that follows somewhere in the distance as the brick walls of the school get smaller.

My socks are soaked through.

I can't feel my toes but I don't stop.

I run faster.

Running to nowhere in particular, just running. Knowing that I would run off the end of the world if I could. But I can't. The cramps in my side remind me that I can't. The broken-glass cuts on my feet let the cold air in and remind me that I have to go somewhere. That I need to stop running soon.

The wet snow makes the bleach drip from my hair and into my eyes. Gives the edges of everything I see the appearance of melting. I wipe away at them but the hills still stay out of focus.

I bend down and fill my palms with white water and wash out my eyes. Blinking until they're clean and the trees are covered with leftover rainbows of chemical poison. Half blind from it but I can see enough to make out the street sign with its familiar address.

I get up and begin to run again.

I only make it a few steps before being grabbed from

behind. The screams that come from my lungs are like the sounds babies make when they squeal so loud their bodies turn red with fever. Screaming at the anticipation of teeth sinking below my skin. Teeth that never come. Only a soft whispering sound like a lullaby blown into the wind.

"Hannah! It's me. It's okay."

His hands are pressed against my stomach like the safe hands of someone alive and I hold on to them. Spin around in his arms and hug him.

Lukas doesn't ask what's wrong. He doesn't ask what happened and lets me cry for a minute into his coat where the nightmare can be swallowed up. Letting the fear fade just enough that I'm able to speak again.

"It happened. Just like you said it would."

"I know," he says. "I was waiting outside the locker room."

I want to tell him I'm sorry. That I should've listened. That I should've believed him no matter how crazy it sounded. If I'd trusted him, maybe none of this would have happened. But I don't get the chance to say any of it because my words are cut off by a ferocious howl coming from the direction of town.

"We have to go," he says, looking over his shoulder. "They're going to come after you once they've gathered everyone. They're going to come and they're going to come fast."

He starts to lead me into the woods and I pull back.

"Wait! I have to go to my house," I tell him. I can tell by his face that he doesn't think it's a smart idea. "If we don't, we won't make it far," pointing to my feet where the blood has seeped through and turned my socks red, pointing at little pink footprints in the snow trailing along the sidewalk from the direction I came.

"Okay, but we have to hurry," he says, already starting to move toward my house.

The snow falls faster as we hurry along the sidewalk. Blanketing the ground and covering the road. Weighing down the branches of the pine trees so that they sag. Draping the empty houses with a coldness that matches the lingering chill of death inside them. Hiding everything under the storm's flakes the same way Maplecrest hides out of sight from the rest of the world.

We round the corner and run up the driveway to my house. Two sets of footprints leaving traces in the snow. But the clouds are getting heavier and the snow is raining down at a faster pace. That should wipe our tracks away. Maybe not soon enough, though—I can hear the sound of an approaching pack in the near distance.

"They're getting closer," I say. I try to open the front door but it's locked. I shake it and push on it but it won't budge. "The key . . . it's in my backpack . . . I left it," I shout in a panic.

Lukas tries the door once but it still doesn't give. I watch as he steps off the porch and picks a rock up from the garden. Before I have time to wonder what he's planning to do, he throws the rock through the front window.

I cover my mouth in surprise as it breaks like fireworks exploding.

Without hesitating, he climbs in and comes around to unlock the door from the inside. "C'mon," he says, keeping an eye on the street for any signs of visitors. "Get what you need and let's go!"

My mind is scattered like the clothes strewn across the floor in my room. The faster I try to find anything, the slower I move. Throwing things about, trying to find shoes or a coat, and finding nothing that I need. Lukas shouts for me from the front door and I'm afraid I'm losing my mind. I put my hands on the sides of my head and squeeze my eyes closed trying to concentrate.

The strong smell of bleach on my fingers wakes me out of my daze and I remember what I need to do.

I need to focus.

The shoes I need are right in front of my face and I slip my injured feet into them. Pull a wool hat over my head to prevent another blinding episode. Then I snatch up the jacket tossed on the bed and listen to the heavy footsteps running down the hall.

Lukas is standing in the doorway as I try to get my arms untangled in the sleeves. "Ready?"

"Yeah, I'm ready," I say and slip past him into the hallway.

The red and blue lights flash against the open door, stopping me in my tracks the way headlights freeze deer to the highway late at night. Reflected off the shards of glass from the broken window, the colors splinter apart and fill the room. Outside they bounce off the warm steel of the police car parked in front of my house.

The sheriff's broad shoulders fill the doorway as he takes one step into my house. Hand resting on his belt, inches from his gun.

"Going somewhere?" he says, removing his sunglasses to

stare at me with the rust-colored eyes of someone who's already dead.

**Sheriff Turner holds** out his hand like he's come to rescue me. "You should just come with me. Make it easy on yourself," he says. "We're your family now."

I cover my ears to muffle the sound of his voice.

"You're not my family," I scream.

The sheriff laughs. A grinding machine-gun laugh that I feel in the hollow center of my bones. "I checked into your past before we recruited you," he says. "You're the perfect candidate for our community. Athletic. Pretty. A desire to be popular. And most important, you have no other family. Not except your dad, but don't worry . . . I've made arrangements for him to join us, too."

"Leave me alone!" I yell.

Lukas grabs my arm. Tells me not to listen to him. Pulling me toward the sliding glass door in the kitchen as the sheriff's stiff boots move without being seen, getting closer without lifting his feet.

"Still a pest, huh?" the sheriff says to Lukas. "I never should've let you make it home the other night. I would've gotten rid of you if I didn't think it would alarm our new cheerleader here. But I suppose you're expendable now. Maybe we could use what's left of you for the football team."

"Piss off!" Lukas sneers.

"If you like, we could use his blood in your boyfriend," he says to me. "Would that makes things easier for you?" Laughing at the suggestion. Laughing at us, at what they're going to do to us. Laughter that sounds like a weapon ringing in my ears as I try and remember to breathe.

A gust of snow blows into the broken window along with the echo of marching zombies. I see a crowd of them coming around the curve. Some dressed like cheerleaders. Some dressed like football players. Others dressed like the people who work in the shops, in the diner, in the pharmacy, and in our school. I cover my mouth so the sheriff won't hear me sob in shock. "The whole town?" I mumble to myself. "The whole town."

"Including us if we don't go right now!" Lukas tells me.

The blast of cold air fills the kitchen when he opens the door. The first figures start to walk up my driveway. I can see Maggie in the front, fingerprints of spilled blood smeared across her face. Meredith, too. And I can see the tiny scratches that split her skin. They don't bleed. They only make the skin pink and sore. Behind them, I see Mrs. Donner and the bug-eyed girl from the pharmacy. The nice waitress from the diner and Coach Johnson. Other teachers, too. And then I see him. I see Greg. He's walking in step with the others. Alongside them with the same expression. With the same ghost eyes and sharp teeth like a grasshopper thirsty to chew my face open.

It dawns on me that he was part of their plan all along. Part of the bait to lure me in. Popularity and a popular boyfriend in return for my life. And I fell for it. I fell for him.

"No," I whisper to myself. Numb and sick to my stomach at the same time. I can't believe I kissed a zombie! I can't believe I put my tongue in a corpse's mouth. That I actually began to love him.

Lukas yanks me toward him and I stumble a step before breaking into a run. There's no time to think about any of this. No time to try to comprehend it as I hear the mob scrambling into my house. Climbing through the windows and through the doors. Coming around the side of the house, too, as we cross my backyard and make for the woods. They keep pace. Never running, but never slowing down. A determined, steady march that will never stop until they catch us.

"I know someplace we can go," Lukas says.

I ignore the pine needles that scrape my bare shins and follow him. Taking a glance back to see how much space there is between us and our pursuers. My eyes catch the sheriff standing at the back door of my house. Letting the others pass by. Letting them do his dirty work as he folds his hands across his chest and watches me run.

"They won't get tired," I say. "I've seen them in practice, they don't ever get tired." The thought terrifies me as I'm already breathing in short, small spurts. The cramps in my side come back to the surface, too, even though I thought I had them buried.

I start to fall behind and Lukas takes my hand. He pulls me at his speed and the trees zip past. The entire forest seems to move for us. Trunks shift out of our way and rocks crawl out of our path. I don't feel the pain in my feet anymore. I don't feel the cold on my cheeks, either. It's like nature is making it easier on us. Like nature wants us to win. And for the first time, I feel like maybe we might survive.

That feeling disappears once we make it up the hill where the crumbling brick walls of an old building stand like a gravestone. Our gravestone as the sun begins to sink behind the hills and the clouds grow black with night.

I raise my eyebrows and my mouth drops open in disbelief.

"Here? This is where you wanted to bring us?"

"What?" Lukas says.

"What? If they somehow manage not to catch us, this place will probably collapse and kill us anyway!"

"No, it won't. Trust me," he says. "I've been through this old factory a million times. There's a place for us to hide."

I bring my hands up to my face and start to bite my nails. "I don't know," I say, eyeing the building as it seems to shiver in the cold. Lukas is already making his way through a fallen section of the wall. Behind me I can hear the snapping twigs. I can sense an army of rust-colored eyes peering through the shadows as they make their way up the hill.

"Okay, I trust you," I say, saying it more to myself than to Lukas since he's already vanished into the belly of the decaying factory.

# SIXTEEN

There's a hole in the ceiling that lets in the last of the twilight and a flurry of snow. In the shadows, I can see Lukas struggling to move a rusted metal container across the floor. It scrapes against the cement with an irritating scream that sends sleeping birds rustling from their sleep. Their wings silhouette against the clouds as they escape through the ceiling.

I mimic them by holding my arms out to my side.

I'd give anything to borrow their magic for just one hour. Praying for my thin arms to sprout feathers and let the wind lift me up, carrying me to safety over the mountains where they'd never follow me.

"Are you going to help me at all?" Lukas says, panting.

I bring my arms back down to my side and blink away the dream of flight. "I don't know what you're trying to do," I say. "I don't even know what we're doing here!"

I look around the small storage room that we've locked ourselves into. The walls are cracked and covered with cobwebs and won't hold up long to the murderous instinct of those creatures. I've seen the kind of strength they have. They will be able to break through in no time.

"Just . . . help me," Lukas stutters, keeping himself from shouting, from losing his temper. "We have to move these things closer together," he explains in a calmer voice.

"Why?" I ask even as I start to help him slide the heavy objects into the center of the room. My hands wipe the dust from the sides. The light from above illuminates a faded sticker of a flame. "What's in these?"

"Some kind of gas," Lukas says. "They used to do something with this stuff up here a long time ago. These few were left behind. They've been here forever."

The first signs that we have visitors can be heard outside the walls. I can feel the ground vibrate from their marching steps. Dust particles rain down and mix with the snowflakes as the building deteriorates.

Lukas ignores it and continues to slide the containers into the center of the room. But I can't. I can't pretend they're not out there. I can't pretend we're safe in here. I grab him by the shoulders and let him see the wild look in my eyes.

"Stop! Just stop!" I scream. "We have to get out of here!"

"NO! Listen to me," he says. "We have to let them in."

"Are you crazy? What are you talking about?"

Lukas shoves his hand in his pocket and pulls out a folded piece of paper. "This! This is what I'm talking about," he says and unfolds the page torn from a comic book showing a hoard of zombies surrounding a girl who looks as scared as

I must look. "This is how they hunt. In a pack. All of them will cram in here to get us."

"Oh, why didn't you say so . . . I feel better already," I bark at him. "Then what happens? This?" I ask, pointing to the other side of the ripped page where the girl's body is torn open. Split down the middle with her organs spilling out. Teeth marks up and down her arms where pieces of her clothes are missing.

Lukas answers me by unscrewing the knob on top of one of the canisters. The gas hisses out and fills the room with the stench of spoiled milk. "We have to open these. They won't be able to smell the gas."

"Did you read that, too?"

"Will you be serious?" he snaps.

"I thought I was," I tell him. "You're the one using a stupid horror comic as our survival guide."

He shakes his head. Asks me again to trust him and I can't help but feel like I'm already trusting him with my life and isn't that enough trust to show for one day. "Look," he says, trying to calm me down while jumping from canister to canister like a rabbit with nimble hands to open the valves. "Once they're all inside the building, we just have to light the gas and blow it up," flashing me the lighter that he brought just in case. Telling me he planned this a long time ago. That he planned it after Alison changed.

"Blow it up? What about us?" I ask. My voice shakes. My hands shake, too, because it all starts to feel so final. Starts to feel so real. Kill or be killed starts to feel real. "How do *we* get out?"

"Over there," he points. "Those stairs go to a basement.

There's a way out through there. We just have to hold them off long enough for the room to fill up with gas, then run out before it collapses."

"How do you know we'll make it?" I ask.

"I don't . . . but I don't think we have a choice," he says.

The door to the room starts to shake as fists begin to pound like hammers on the other side. Lukas rushes over there. He piles anything he can find in front of it. An empty filing cabinet. A broken chair. Anything that might slow them down as I hurry to open the rest of the valves and pollute the air with the hissing sound of an explosive future.

The door isn't the only way they try to get in. There's a rumbling against every thin wall in the office. A drumming like the marching band during the football games. A steady rain of fists that threaten to break in. A threat they make good on once I see the first hand reach through the plaster.

Vacant eyes stare back at me, crazed with the taste for blood on their tongue. Another hand breaks through. Another pale face with deep blue veins pulsing as it reaches for me. Growling like an animal in a cage.

"LUKAS!" I scream.

"Go!" he yells, holding the door that has been opened a crack. Several arms push through the space between it and the wall. One of them wears the brown sleeve of a police officer. A sheriff's stripes sewn onto the side.

"Not by myself!" I shout.

I'm not leaving him here.

I'm not leaving him to these animals.

He can tell I'm not going anywhere until he comes, too, so he pushes off the door and it swings open in a violent push. Lukas runs toward me, shoving me into motion. I look behind me as we get to the basement door. The sheriff is lumbering into the room with what looks like a hundred zombies right behind.

**My sneakers splash** through the water collected on the basement floor. I can see the glimmer of nightfall through a doorway ahead of me and keep running toward it as Lukas stays behind me. He's trying to block the next door in their path, the last obstacle before they can pull our limbs apart. The only way in since even they can't punch their way through cinder-block walls.

Lukas secures the dead bolt.

A click of safety that buys at least a few minutes.

"Come on, we'll have to start the fire from outside," he says.

He steps in front of me, steps up to our exit. The promise of freedom once he opens the door, only the door opens even before he is able to turn the handle. Opens from the outside where Maggie stands backlit like a monster from a child's nightmare. A few streaks of her blond hair are all that's visible outside the shadows.

"We didn't finish, Madison," she growls. "We're not done until I say we're done." Her voice is distorted and ugly. When she turns her head into the light, I can see pink sores have spread across the porcelain skin of her face. I've noticed it with all of them. All the pretty cheerleaders turning into all the pretty zombies. I saw it with Greg, too, his boyish face more disfigured by the minute.

The more they need to feed, the more their beauty fades. Another symptom of the death sickness.

Lukas charges at her. Attempts to knock her back and clear the way, but she doesn't budge. When they collide, he's the one who gets the worst of it. Her hands clutch his shoulders and even with the loud banging behind me I can hear the crunch of his bones, being crushed in her fists like a vice.

I bring my hands up to cover my face as she tosses him aside like throwing away a strangled puppy. "What do you want?" My words muffled as I speak into my hands. Scared and small and caught between sobs as I hear Lukas trying his best to handle the pain of broken bones with his silent screams.

"You can still have everything," Maggie says with the splash of her feet moving toward me. "It will just take a second and then it's over. You'll be popular and beautiful forever."

"Beautiful?" I shout. "Look at you! You're not beautiful! None of you are beautiful!"

Her hands snatch at me. Strike like lightning and her fingers come up with a clump of my hair that hung down under my hat. She tugs harder and my neck bends back from the force as I fall to my knees in the filthy water.

"It will just take a second," she growls. "You'll barely feel it."

Grabbing tighter, she stretches my skin until I'm forced to lean my neck back and stare up at her. I reach behind me to hold on to her wrist and keep her from ripping the scalp from my skull. Letting the pain escape through hurried breaths from my open mouth as the flutter of my heartbeat strains to keep up with my fear, pounding in rhythm with the blunt sound of fists beating against the metal door as those animals try to force their way in.

Maggie doesn't need their help because I'm helpless against her.

Helpless to stop her from completing what she wants done to me.

I watch as she brings her other hand up to her neck and tilts her head to the side. Making her fingers like claws, she digs her nails deep into her pale skin. Pulls down violently like a razor, painting four red streaks that reach from behind her ear to the base of her neck. A trickle of blood leaking from each like worms from rotten meat.

"A few drops is all it takes to change you," she says. "My blood will infect the rest of your blood. It will eat away at that pathetic girl you call Hannah. Erase her completely. Then you'll become something more perfect, like us. Stronger. Prettier. Better."

I shake my head but she pulls on my hair harder, snapping my head back like tugging on the strings of a puppet. I feel her breath on my face as she leans over me. Drops of blood drip from her wounds, inches from my face. I close my mouth, but Maggie cups my chin in her hand. Squeezing my cheeks until my teeth begin to shift and I have no choice but to open it again.

"Don't be so nervous," she says. "You're going to like this. You're finally going to have what you've always wanted. You're going to be adored."

I try to scream out but my jaw is locked in place by her

fingers and my tongue cannot make a sound without me being able to move it.

Everything goes dark as her hair drapes across my face.

My lips brush against her cheek as her skin slides over them like a snake sliding over sand. I feel the bones in her cheek turn into the bones of her jaw. The hollow space before my lips touch again against her neck. And I hold my breath anticipating the warm taste of disease about to touch inside me . . . to kill me.

A quick swipe of created wind stops everything.

The dull sound of metal meeting bone.

The blow travels down her spine and vibrates through her fingertips, passing from her body to mine as she releases me. Releases me too soon. Releases me while I'm still clean . . . while I'm still me.

I open my eyes and see Lukas standing behind her.

The heavy pipe in his hand is stained with the skid marks of bone and bleached hair. Swung with the last force left in the torn muscles of both his shoulders. Enough strength left to open a gash in the back of her head that keeps her from getting up.

New lines form in his face as he winces in pain, dropping the weapon into the still water around his ankles. I get up as quickly as I can. Rush over to him and wrap my hands around his waist to keep him from collapsing as his body goes numb.

I drag him through the stagnant water, resting at the small set of steps that lead out the open door where the world is new and white and safe as the snow that covers it. I crawl behind him and slip my arms under his the way rescuers do when they pull people from burning cars. And from one step to the next, I make his body move with mine toward safety.

But safety is farther than the touch of falling snow.

Safety isn't as simple as a locked door bending under the pursuit of maddened flesh eaters. Safety doesn't come with the fragments of bone split open to show us her skull. Because the undead don't die the way they should. They don't die until they are destroyed, until all the life is burned out of them. So Maggie gets to her feet before we're able to get to wherever safe is.

I struggle to pull Lukas up the last step and through the door as Maggie drags herself through the grime. Injured but still dangerous, still deadly. Her eyes, rolled back in her head, still glow with a faint color of toxic rust. Teeth like razors when she flashes a smile. Grip like a snare trap when she digs her hands into Lukas's ankles.

"You can watch me devour your friend," she growls. "A little preview of what you're soon going to enjoy."

The skin peels off his ankle as easily as the rind from ripe fruit and there's nothing I can do to stop it. No matter how hard I pull, his body doesn't budge. And when he looks in my eyes, we both know I can't save him.

His fingers slide into my palm even as Maggie moves in to tear him open the way I've been torn open in dreams. I start to cry the way I haven't cried since I was little as I feel the lighter pass from his hand to mine. I finally see what I should have seen that day in the lunchroom the first time he looked at me. I see that he is good. That he cares about me. And when he tells me, "Go!" is when I know that he will die because of me.

The skin around his eyes turns pink.

The pupils shine the color of the sky before fading into rust.

His hand falls in slow motion like the snow around my face as I back away. Wiping my eyes that won't stop filling with tears. Shaking my arms free from the sleeves of my jacket as I sob. Pulling the sweater off over my head, leaving only a T-shirt to protect me. I let the spark of the flame touch the *M* and let the fabric burn as I run around to the side of the building.

It leaves my hand and takes flight.

Trailing through the night sky like a shooting star and I wish for the worst to happen as the air begins to catch fire. Sparks igniting sparks until I'm blinded by an explosion as bright as the sun landing in the forest.

Blown back from the blast, my body falls like an angel softly against the snow.


When I open my eyes, I'm surrounded by the warm glow of burning bodies that had been dead since long ago. I watch the halo of fire where the building once stood and I can't help but notice how pretty the flames are with the falling snow. Watching the way the flames climb over one another to be the first to touch the sky.

And I watch the bricks fall the way snowflakes fall.

Collapsing at random.

Drowning the beasts trapped inside.

And I almost wish I could hear them choking on the incinerated air. The sound of them dying like the most beautiful song ever sung by the wind. Squealing as they try to slither through the cracks until their last unnatural breath is cut off in a last gasp.

"D-

"E-

"A-

"T-

"H-

"DEATH!

"DEATH!

"DEATH!"

I scream the chant at the top of my lungs. Stomping my feet to the cadence. My mouth moving mechanically until the words break apart and begin to come out only in fragments.

I sit down in the snow and let myself cry the way I've wanted to for hours. Crying until my nose runs. Crying until the wind freezes the tears against my face. Until my clothes are soaked through and my skin turns red as my body begins to shiver violently to fight off frostbite.

I make myself stand up.

"Just go, Hannah," I tell myself as I hear sirens screaming on the other side of the hill. I don't know if there are more of them. If there are other zombies left in town to come up here to help. Coming here to finish me off. I don't know, but I know I don't want to stay and see for myself. I don't want to stay another second in this place.

I walk past the running engine of the sheriff's abandoned police car, the sirens still shining a silent rotation of blue and red lights that are swallowed up by the blaze. I walk past the basement door that I escaped from, but it isn't there anymore. Replaced with a pile of brick like everything else.

I walk back to the spot in the woods where we came from. Me and Lukas, but there's only me now to follow the moonlight back to my house.

Walking away from the roar of fire engines.

Walking away from the heat of the explosion and into the cold of the trees where I will wear its safe darkness all around me.

I focus on the way the branches crisscross my path, thin lines slicing through my vision like the thin scratches they will make against my bare arms. I focus on the shadows that stretch as far as I can see because of the brightness behind me. I focus on anything that will make my mind blank like the clouds that crawl in front of the moon. Anything that will keep me from thinking about Lukas and how I left him to die in my place.

The snow has already covered the tracks of marching footprints through my backyard and erased all traces of being chased. Vanished like the victims that used to fill the empty houses on every street. The broken window in my front room and the mud dragged across the kitchen floor from wet shoes are the only signs that anything happened here.

I ignore them and walk over to close the front door.

Pull the curtain to close off the draft.

Slide my feet over the wet floor to the bathroom and turn the hot water on in the shower. I don't bother slipping out of my clothes before climbing in. Before letting the water wash over me and bring a tingling feeling back to my hands and feet.

I can see myself in the mirror as I lean against the tile. All the color has drained from my face. All the color has drained from my hair, too, and I look more like one of them than myself. Look more dead than alive as I slowly let myself slip down the side of the wall and sit in the tub.

The phone rings in the hallway.

My father's voice on the answering machine tells me he got held up. That he won't be back tonight like he planned. He won't be home until the morning and I curl my knees up to my chest and hold them there. Rest my head in my arms and close my eyes.

Tomorrow it will all be gone.

Tomorrow.

# SEVENTEEN

**I open the front door and stand on the porch in my nightshirt.**
I don't remember sleeping or waking, but at some point night
became morning and I missed it.

The sun has already melted the snow from the blacktop.
Water drips off the roof above my head and sounds like
birds chirping as it runs through the storm gutters.

I watch the car inch along Walnut Cove. The familiar
stuttering of its engine comforts me. The rust stains in the
paint remind me of soft, spotted stuffed animals and don't
embarrass me the way they have so many times before, sitting in the passenger's seat. They used to feel like black eyes
as we drove through towns. Telltale scars of how poor we
are and how much I didn't fit in with the kids who got
everything they wanted simply by asking for it. But I don't
care about any of that anymore. None of that matters as my
dad pulls into the driveway, because seeing the car parked

there is like coming back to life, a little piece of something normal.

He waves at me through the car window and I run out to meet him. Running over the wet cement in my bare feet, unconcerned about the cuts opening up again or the cold that turns my toes bright red. Running toward him the way survivors run to their rescuers in the movies, throwing my arms around him before he has the chance to steady himself and we both fall back against the car.

"Glad to see you, too," my dad says, laughing.

I only bury my face further into his coat and hold him tighter. Holding him long enough for the steam of our breath to rise up and become part of the clouds. Pressing my face against him hard enough to where everything goes black and somehow wishing I could hide there forever.

My dad lets go of me and holds his arms out to the side, letting me know it's okay for me to stop hugging him. I pull back a little bit and look him in the eyes. I see myself there, looking up at him. I see the swollen skin under my eyes from staying awake all night staring at the bathroom tile and all the color stripped from my hair and my complexion. My reflection is Madison's reflection and I realize just how close I came to becoming her.

"Is everything okay?" my dad asks. Wrinkles appear in his forehead as he looks at me, really looking for the first time. "What did you do to your hair?" he asks, his fingers touching at the blond streaks that have made each strand brittle and dead like those who made it that way.

I'd thought about it all morning. I thought about how I was going to tell him what happened but there is no good place to start. No sane way to tell him all the things that have gone wrong. So I say the only thing that makes sense to me. "You're late," I say.

My dad laughs again. He tells me the same thing he's told me for years, how sometimes he's not sure which of us is the parent and which is the child. Normally I would snap at him. I'd tell him the uncertainty was because parents aren't supposed to leave their teenage daughters to fend for themselves for almost two weeks. But I realize that some things don't matter anymore. Getting mad at him for something that cannot be changed is one of them, so I stay silent, shivering in the cold.

My dad leans into the backseat to retrieve the bags lying across it. I keep glancing around for any signs of strangers watching us. For any hidden spies in the scenery studying us. Hunting us. Waiting for just the right moment to strike, because I know deep in the pit of my stomach that it isn't over. I can sense it. I know there are more of them running around. Lurking behind every vacant window of every house for sale, just waiting to take the places left behind by those who burned in the fire.

"There was some kind of commotion in town," my dad says.

I didn't let him finish.

"Dad, we have to leave," I say. The fear in my voice is fresh. A new fear. A fear of being discovered. Knowing that they will find out I'm not dead. They will find out what I did, that I killed the others.

My dad smiles in the confident way he always does when he thinks I'm overreacting. "It's nothing to worry about," he assures me. "Just some sort of accident at an old plant." He comes over to me and puts an arm lightly on my shoulder. He says it was just a fire. That no one got hurt.

"No one got hurt?" I ask, terrified that an army of vengeful, badly burned cheerleaders will suddenly come marching up our street behind the blare of police sirens.

"That's what the deputy sheriff told me," he says. "But they did have to cancel the school's football game because of it. He said the fire department needed to use the parking lot for a staging area."

"Deputy?" I ask.

"Yeah, that's the other good news I have," he says. "It seems there's an opening right here in the police department. I guess they're looking for a new sheriff and once I told him about my qualifications, he told me I should apply. I might actually get to be a cop again. Wouldn't that be something?"

"Yeah," I mumble, too distracted trying to figure out what's going on to argue.

Slowly I begin to piece it together. What the deputy told my dad about no one getting hurt is a lie. So is the excuse about the game. There is no game today because there is no team. There is no sheriff because he was in that building. They are lying to cover it up because they know what the others were. They all must know or they'd be asking questions. They'd want to know what happened to everyone else, all the new missing people of Maplecrest.

Maybe they've already been replaced.

Maybe nothing has changed.

Maybe they still want me. Maybe if they make my dad

the new sheriff, they think they will be able to make me the new Maggie.

"Dad, listen to me," I plead. "You can't take that job! We've got to get out of here!" I start pulling him into the house. Telling him that I'll get my stuff and be ready to go in a few minutes. That we have to go now before it's too late.

"Hannah, what's got into you?"

"You're not listening to me!" I shout. "We have to move!"

My dad grabs hold of me and keeps me still.

"We're not moving anymore," and when he speaks, his tone is firm and strict in a way I've never heard it sound before. "This is our chance to make a home."

I shake my head. The tears start over again, coming as freely as if they'd never stopped from the night before. "No," I whisper. "No, it's not."

"It is!" he yells, raising his voice at me for the first time I can remember.

I pull free, still shaking my head. Searching his eyes for any sign telling if they already got to him. If he's already not my dad anymore. I back away from him, backing toward the house as he starts to talk again. Calmer. As if he notices a mistake he might have made.

"Hannah, listen to me," he says. "You know how you get when I've been gone like this. Your imagination runs wild with all sorts of ideas. That's why I'm doing this. For you. You won't have to go through that again."

He walks toward me, holding his hands out like I'm something fragile that he needs to handle delicately or I will shatter.

"It's different this time," I say. "I swear."

"You're right, this time we're staying."

My legs give out under me and I have to lean against the front door to stand up. Covering my mouth to keep the screams from flooding out. Letting only the whimper of tears choke through as my dad begins to run his fingers through my hair.

"Think how nice it will be not to run anymore," he says. "You won't have to worry about starting a new school or making new friends. We'll be happy here. I can finally do something that I enjoy and you won't have to quit the cheerleading squad that you told me about."

I turn my head to look at him when he says the last part. Something about the way he says it. Something like he knows. And when my eyes meet his, I expect to see them shining with the bright blue spark of electricity of someone already infected because, sooner or later, we will all become zombies in this town.

# Go Fish!

# GO**FISH**

## BRIAN JAMES

### What did you want to be when you grew up?

Like most kids my age, I wanted to be a Jedi Knight, or space smuggler with my own spaceship and a furry alien as a best friend. Alas, technology didn't advance as rapidly as my imagination anticipated.

### When did you realize you wanted to be a writer?

I was around eleven years old when I started wanting to be a writer. It was sort of an odd desire considering that, at the time, I didn't really like to read all that much. But I loved coming up with stories that I used to create while playing with action figures. I'd set up these elaborate plots that would take days and days for me to play out. Around that age is when I began to have the urge to write these stories down.

### What's your most embarrassing childhood memory?

When I was in fifth grade, my best friend tape-recorded a phone conversation where I admitted to liking a certain girl. Of course, I knew he was recording it. It was actually a plan that we came up with together. The second part of the plan was getting him to play it for everyone at recess. It seemed easier to admit that I liked her if I could pretend I was being betrayed. However, that didn't make it any less embarrassing when the whole fifth grade heard it the next day. The girl handled it with class, which only made me like her more.

**As a young person, who did you look up to most?**
My mother. She did everything.

**What was your worst subject in school?**
I was lucky enough not to have any "bad" subjects. I always did well in school. But, ironically, my worst subject was definitely Spelling. I'm still a horrible speller, so I'm very thankful for spell check.

**What was your best subject in school?**
Probably math and science, though I never really enjoyed either of them. But for some reason, they both came easily to me. English classes took much more effort on my part, which is most likely why they kept my interest.

**What was your first job?**
Babysitting. I have two younger brothers and two younger sisters. So I was a de facto babysitter very often. But my first real job was as a lifeguard when I was a teenager. I also taught swimming lessons to toddlers; the patience required for that job certainly helped prepare me to be a writer.

**How did you celebrate publishing your first book?**
Honestly, I'm still celebrating. Every time I look at any of my books, I'm very thankful.

**Where do you write your books?**
I have an office in my house where I do all of my work. The room is filled with books, music, and toys. All the walls are covered with photos, pictures from magazines, drawings I've done, and letters from kids . . . it's sort of like an external portrait of what goes on in my head.

**Where do you find inspiration for your writing?**
Anywhere and everywhere. I get inspiration from other art, be it music, literature, film, or visual art. I also find inspiration in the world around me. Any little thing can be inspiring if you take the time to look at it. I like to keep a notebook on me at all times and write down ideas because I never know when a passing stranger or a bit of conversation will spark my imagination.

**Which of your characters is most like you?**
In varying degrees, all of my characters are somewhat based on me, or aspects of my personality. However, Brendon from *Pure Sunshine* is very much me. It's the most autobiographical book I've written.

**When you finish a book, who reads it first?**
My wife is always the first person to read anything I write. After she reads it, I usually do another draft before anyone else ever sees it.

**Are you a morning person or a night owl?**
Certainly NOT a morning person . . . in my younger days, I'd say I was a night owl. Though now, I'm solidly a day person.

**What's your idea of the best meal ever?**
A twenty-course dinner with every kind of food . . . so much food that I'd explode if I ate it all. There'd have to be Asian food,

Hispanic food, seafood, gourmet dishes, and good old American cuisine like pizza, burgers, and fries. Then I'd wash it all down with a sundae of chocolate chip ice cream, hot fudge, peanut butter topping, whipped cream and one of those fake cherries on top.

### Which do you like better: cats or dogs?
Growing up, I was always a dog person. I had two dogs as a child. Now I have two cats. I could never choose between the two. They're both so different and both have so much to offer.

### What do you value most in your friends?
Intellect and open-mindedness.

### Where do you go for peace and quiet?
I live in a remote part of the Catskills, so there's no lack of peace and quiet. If I'm feeling even more in need of seclusion, a long hike through the mountains is as good as it gets.

### What makes you laugh out loud?
Junie B. Jones, Homer Simpson, and *It's Always Sunny in Philadelphia*.

### What's your favorite song?
I'm a music junkie and have a collection of a few thousand CDs, so choosing a favorite song might be the hardest task for me to imagine. I couldn't even tell you my favorite album without naming at least twenty or so.

### Who is your favorite fictional character?
Addie Pray from *Paper Moon*.

**What are you most afraid of?**
Any evil that cloaks itself in an elaborate disguise.

**What time of year do you like best?**
Winter. I love cold, grey, snowy weather and always have. I've read that people most enjoy the season they were born in . . . at least for me, that theory holds true.

**What's your favorite TV show?**
I think *Lost* is the most creative show on the air. So many television shows assume viewers are dumb. It's one of the few shows that assumes its viewers are smart and can handle big ideas. I'm also a nut for *Doctor Who* and *Battlestar Galactica*.

**If you were stranded on a desert island, who would you want for company?**
My wife. We've never run out of things to say and she's the only person I've ever met whose company I never grow tired of at any point.

**If you could travel in time, where would you go?**
The future . . . WAY in the future . . . as far as it would take for long-distance space travel to be possible.

**What's the best advice you have ever received about writing?**
Strangely enough, it wasn't meant to be advice. A teacher (not one of mine) tried to discourage me from pursing writing because he said there were only about a thousand people that could make a living as a writer and asked if I really thought I was one of them. I thought about it for a second and decided that, yes, I did think I was one of them. And whenever I've felt discouraged, I remember that conversation and it always helps

me regain my confidence. I think in order to achieve anything, you need first believe that you can.

## What do you want readers to remember about your books?

Whatever is important to them. I think that's the great thing about art. It's a fulfillment of personal creativity that people respond to their own personal way. For me, what readers take away from my books isn't too important. As long as the book is meaningful to them in some way, that's all that matters to me. That the book has some personal meaning for them is the greatest compliment a writer can get.

## What would you do if you ever stopped writing?

Probably teach, though I'm not sure I'd like it . . . so I'm going to hope it never comes to that.

## What do you like best about yourself?

The fact that I've never completely lost the ability to be a child.

## What is your worst habit?

Smoking. It's such a disgusting habit that I've been able to scale back but never quite kick. My biggest regret in life is that I ever started.

## What is your best habit?

I'm a clean person without being a freak about it.

## What do you consider to be your greatest accomplishment?

I like to think I haven't reached my greatest accomplishment yet. I still believe that the best work I've done is always the latest. By never feeling that I've accomplished anything, it keeps me motivated to keep striving.

**Where in the world do you feel most at home?**
New York City. I lived there for ten years before I moved away for a variety of reasons. But anytime I'm ever there, I feel that I belong.

**What do you wish you could do better?**
Sing. I'd give anything to be able to sing.

**What would your readers be most surprised to learn about you?**
I'm not-so-distantly related to Jesse James.

*K*eep reading for an excerpt from
## Brian James's **The Heights**,
*available now in hardcover from Feiwel and Friends.*

# EXCERPT

Always near the bay, I've felt like a fish. Pushed along through every day of my life the way fish are by the currents. Not caring much where the streams take me..never struggling this way or that. I'm fine with just drifting forward..moving in and out of the sunbeams like the cars move in and out of the fog on the city's highways. Never sure where I'm going..just that I'm going somewhere different than where I am.

Catherine says I feel that way because I was born in March..because I'm a water sign.

I asked her once what that had to do with anything.

—It has everything to do with everything, Henry— she told me. —It's the reason you're the way you are. Everything is written in the stars— saying it like it was the easiest thing in the world to understand because that's the way Catherine is..any question can be figured out by whatever idea pops into her head first.

The way I think of things is never as direct as hers..more like the rise and fall of the tide before the water breaks against the rocks. Always like the waves brought by a storm..like how there's too much water and not enough space. My feelings fight inside me like that. Push up against each other..pushing one out of the way to let another take over.

I feel it happening now as I watch Catherine walking out of our school. My nervousness giving way to something better when I see the wind pick up off the bay like it's attracted to her. The sun clears away the clouds, lifts the shadows, and gives a warm color to her skin. I haven't been waiting more than five minutes, but it still feels like I've been waiting my whole life. Every day feels like that.. like I only exist for her.

She tucks her hair away from the breeze and waves to me all in one slight and simple motion that blends so easily with her smile.. her eyes pulling me toward her like a magnet as I push myself away from the tree I'm leaning against. It's only once I start toward her that I see she's not alone. There's a group of her friends trailing behind her.. after her.. crowding her like a net strangling a butterfly.

I'm not sure *friends* is the right word to call them.. more like parasites. Except Nelly, not one of them care about her.. or about one another. They just care about making her just like them.. a survival instinct to increase their number of clones. They don't see that she's special in any way. They don't even want her to be special. They want her to be the same.. want everyone to be the same. I can't stand when she's around them.. the way they make her feel like shit for being different.. for being better.

She never sees it like that.

She needs me to see it for her.. to keep her safe from their popularity traps.. from the people who just want to strip away all the beautifully strange parts that make her the most perfect girl in the world.

I feel the shift inside me again.. the waves swaying as my feet stomp the ground with an angry pace. I clench my hands until my fingers turn white.. my eyes screaming as I walk up to her but keeping the rest of me calm because she hates when I'm mean. I have to do my best to hide it.. to play nice.. play along just until I can get her away.

It's not so hard. Around her I can usually stay calm just by glancing over at her every few seconds. Catherine's always been able to settle me down like that.

—Hey, you ready?— I ask.. cutting into the middle of the conversation and getting a series of nasty looks in return from everyone except her. But even Catherine's smile softens.. disappears almost completely when she turns to the other girls and tells them she'll see them tomorrow. — C'mon— I say.. taking her hand in mine.

I feel better once we're walking away.. once we're alone. I always do. I don't know why being alone with her makes such a difference.. why I can't be myself unless it's just us. Maybe it would be different if I'd been born in the winter like her. Maybe if I were a Capricorn like Catherine, I wouldn't get so crazy about things the way I sometimes do. Everything would be —*perfectly reasonable*— just how she always says it is.

But then again, if I wasn't the way I am.. and if she wasn't the way she is.. maybe we wouldn't be so perfect for each other.

—*It's the reason we get along so well*— Catherine's always telling me. She says our astrological signs are compatible.. that the earth needs the water just like we need each other.

I love the sound of her voice when she says —*We need each other*— I hear it in my head as we walk away the last of the afternoon.. playing it back over and over as the clouds linger above the path leading us through Fort Point Park.. her fingers between mine and even though we don't say a thing, I can still hear the words she's told me nearly every day since the day we met. —*We need each other*—

I don't remember much about that day, but I remember the cold. It found its way into the center of my bones like a ghost passing through my skin. I remember being alone.. wandering the city by myself until her father found me —*Where's your mother, son?*— he asked but I was too frozen to answer. I didn't know the answer. I'm not sure there was an answer because I'm not sure that I wasn't born on that day.. born five years old and shivering.

I can remember him gathering me in his arms and carrying me to his car. I remember the headlights cutting through the night like the glowing eyes of an overgrown insect. Then he brought me to his house and I saw her standing at the top of the stairs. I remember her perfectly. I remember her hair was like a sunset drawn with red crayons. And when she smiled at me, her face was warm. It was the first time the cold ever left me.

Catherine was different than anyone else in the world. I knew it just by staring at her. She wasn't just another girl..more like a star plucked from the sky and trapped between tiny bones..a star capturing heat that I could hold on to for warmth. My very own star that I knew would guide me forever as long as I held on tight and never let go. It's the only thing I've ever understood as easily as she seems to understand everything.

—Henry? What are you thinking about? I mean right now, what are you thinking about?— she asks me suddenly. Her voice always has a way of pulling me back from my thoughts..pulling me toward her no matter how far away I've drifted.

I hold her hand a little tighter as we walk.

—You know..just about things— I say.

She smiles softly like the dawn. —I think I do— she says.

The air fills with the sudden sound of cars driving on the Golden Gate Bridge, suspended high above as we pass under. Once we're on the other side, we'll start to climb up the hill that will bring us just as high..alongside Baker Beach and all the way down to Sea Cliff Avenue where our home sits a few yards from the steep rocks that look down into the ocean. Until then, we're alone. The entire city of San Francisco fades away behind us. The school day disappears into the past. Nothing exists except Catherine and me walking together like we've done every day that I can remember.

She glances over at the wind whipping across the brown surface of the water in the distance. A flock of gulls take off like balloons set free from a child's hand, floating forever up to heaven when the gust hits. Catherine watches them like they're something made of magic.

Her hair gets swept across her face and I watch her hands tuck the longer strands behind her ears. It slides through her palm the same as it did the night we met .. still the same motion of her wrist at sixteen as she had when we were five.

—Do you ever wonder what it would be like to be with them?— she asks.

—Be like with who?— I ask. Her eyes wander up to the sky, borrowing the color from it. I know then that she means the birds. —The seagulls?— I say .. thinking as I talk .. imagining myself in flight. —I don't think it would be much different from this— I tell her. —I mean, it would be different just because we were flying .. but I doubt it would feel any different—

I can see her tongue pushing against the inside of her cheek the way it always does when she's thinking. She considers my opinion for as long as it takes to climb up the last steep hill before the path flattens again, giving us a perfect glimpse of the taller buildings that peek in and out between the trees .. the downtown buildings that always draw your eyes to the pyramid rising higher than the rest. Catherine stares at it for a moment before spinning around to face me again. —But how could it not feel different?— she asks. Her words sound small and curious. Then she pulls her hand away from mine and stops walking as if standing still will help her understand. She places her hands on her hips .. leans her weight on one leg and demands that I either agree with her or give a better answer.

I struggle for words .. trying to let my thoughts settle into little pools that are easier to collect than waves. It's easier to think when she's around..easier to steady the storm. —*Well*— I say— I mean..it's like if you were a bird..and I was a bird..we'd still be you and me just with wings and feathers and stuff like that. But we'd still be us..we'd still be talking about this, just the other way around—

Catherine narrows her eyes. She studies me and I can almost see her trying to work out what I've said. —Okay, I guess that sort of makes sense— she says. She takes my hand again and starts walking again. — But I still think it would be different— she tells me. —I think I'd feel dizzy always going up so high and swooping back down—

She starts laughing and I can't help but smile. We've always been contagious to each other in that way. I've never doubted that it's why Mr. Earnshaw let me stay..let me grow up as one of the family and gave me his last name even though Earnshaw means wealthy and Caucasian and I was just a scrawny orphan with Mexican skin. He did it because I've always been able to make Catherine smile and he's just as addicted to her smile as I am.

The sun breaks in and out of the leaves as we walk..the shadows of so many trees dancing under our feet. I steal glances at Catherine but she's gone somewhere else..staring off into the horizon like she's trying to memorize the different shades of copper blue that streak the sky. She only comes back because I squeeze her hand tighter..bringing her closer to me..a reflex that happens whenever the breeze catches the faint scent of soap from her skin.

Her body goes soft like she's just waking up..her chin resting on her shoulder when she looks at me..facing the sun so that her freckles fade in the glare, asking me if she's drifted off again.

I nod. —Don't worry about it—

Catherine takes a deep breath..stretching out her arms as she comes alive. —You know what Mrs. Crane said today?— she asks. I shake my head. Mrs. Crane is our homeroom teacher and Catherine's physics teacher and is capable of saying just about anything..most of it guaranteed to be insane. —She said I daydream too much— Catherine tells me.

—That's because she's crazy— I say and we both laugh..but mine is fake..half fake anyway because what I'm really thinking is how I'd like to run back there and tell Mrs. Crane what a lousy bitch I think she is.

—Yeah, I guess— Catherine says but she lowers her head..keeps her eyes on the ground as her shoes step over stray leaves. —You don't think she's right, do you?— she asks, suddenly looking at me.

—Are you serious?— A hint of anger in my voice because I hate when she doubts herself..when all the things other people say creep in and make her forget how much better than them she really is. It's why I have to protect her..shield her from all the bullshit the world throws at us.

Her mouth forms the shape of a question when she bites her bottom lip..she shrugs her shoulder and saying —Maybe— She says sometimes she gets so completely lost in what she's thinking about that it's like she disappears. —Does that make me weird?—

—I don't think you should worry about anything Crazy Crane says— I tell her and she tells me that's not what she means..not really anyway. —Then what are you talking about?— I ask.

—I don't know..nothing I guess— she says. —It's just..sometimes I think I should pay more attention to things..try to be more like everyone else, you know?—

—No. I don't— I tell her honestly. —Being like everyone else is boring. Besides..you're interesting and they all suck—

She smiles differently then..a secret smile when she says —thanks— and begins swinging her arms..playfully digging her elbow into my side..letting me know I've said enough to stop her from worrying for now.

We see the house as soon as we reach the sidewalk. The steepled roof catches the light, making it look like a house out of a fairy tale. Not that every house in the Heights doesn't already look that way.. each with its own view of the cliffs where the sidewalks fall into the ocean.. with their endless mazes of rooms and expensive furniture.. but there's something about ours that seems better and makes all the others fade into the scenery. Maybe it's the soft white color that seems to hold on to the twilight even after the sun has set.. or maybe it's the large windows on the fourth floor that look into Catherine's room on one side and mine on the other. Or maybe it's just because it's home.

Whatever it is, I've always thought our house was really Heaven in disguise. Sometimes instead of thinking I was born the day Mr. Earnshaw found me, I think it's really the day I died. But either way it doesn't matter.. dead or alive doesn't matter.. as long as every day ends with me being washed up on its porch, I'll be fine. Because as long as there's the house, there will always be Catherine.

Nothing else will ever mean anything to me.